The Secret Church

Books by Louise A. Vernon

Title	Subject
The Beggars' Bible	John Wycliffe
The Bible Smuggler	William Tyndale
Doctor in Rags	Paracelsus and Hutterites
A Heart Strangely Warmed	John Wesley
Ink on His Fingers	Johann Gutenberg
Key to the Prison	George Fox and Quakers
The King's Book	King James Version, Bible
The Man Who Laid the Egg	Erasmus
Night Preacher	Menno Simons
Peter and the Pilgrims	English Separatists, Pilgrims
The Secret Church	Anabaptists
Thunderstorm in Church	Martin Luther

The Secret Church

Louise A. Vernon
Illustrated by Allan Eitzen

Herald
Press

Scottdale, Pennsylvania
Waterloo, Ontario

CONTENTS

1

INTO THE NIGHT

HUNGRY from herding cattle all day, twelve-year-old Richard Janssen ran home to supper. Neither Father nor Mother had returned from mending field boundaries. Richard started the fire in the kitchen fireplace and set the big iron kettle of soup on the grate.

A sharp knock at the farmhouse door startled him. Who would be visiting Father and Mother this late in the day? He opened the door and saw a girl facing the road. Her shoulders shook with muffled sobs. Richard recognized Trudi Schwartz, the motherless daughter of the most hated man in the church parish.

"Why, Trudi, what's the matter? Are you afraid to go home?"

Trudi wiped her eyes with her short, pleated apron. "They're coming this way. I was on my way home, and I saw them coming. I can't bear it—the cries of the children."

At first Richard did not understand. "They've been helping their folks work on the field boundries like everybody else this time of year. Children always squabble when they're tired. They'll forget all about it as soon as they're home."

Trudi stared at him, reproach in her brown eyes. "That's not it at all, Richard. Don't you understand? It's those Anabaptist people. They're being stoned out of Münster." She burst into tears.

Several families stumbled past the farmhouse. Behind them a group of men rained clods and stones on the defenseless outcasts. Mothers hugged babies close. Fathers with outstretched arms herded the little ones ahead. Richard heard the high-pitched cries of frightened children and the harsh, angry voices of the men. He saw the violent thrusts of their arms, and the sight sickened him.

He choked with pity and fought down a nauseating horror, but he did not dare admit his sympathy. The dreaded Anabaptists were people who had turned against the church, and they had to be punished.

He pulled Trudi into the house. "Don't look any more. You mustn't listen, and you mustn't feel sorry for them. You know that, don't you, Trudi?"

Tears streamed down Trudi's face. She brushed them away with an angry gesture. "Richard Janssen, how can you be so unfeeling? Those people out there are just like us. Who has the right to stone them out of their homes? Who? Tell me that."

"Now, Trudi, you know very well that the church has the right. These people are—they are—"

"Yes, I know. Say it. Heretics. And heretics are to be banished, excommunicated, or killed.

But the Anabaptists believe in God, so who says they are to be persecuted? Does God say so?"

"I suppose so, Trudi." Richard checked himself. "I mean, I hadn't thought about it." Trudi's question bothered him. Not knowing what to say, he stirred the soup vigorously with a long-handled spoon.

Trudi pushed his hand and the spoon clattered to the floor. "It's time you started thinking about something besides filling your stomach, Richard. I've been doing a lot of thinking since Mother died."

"But God doesn't want you to think. He wants you to obey." Even as he said the words, Richard realized how ridiculous they sounded. Surely God meant for people to think, or why would He have given them minds?

Trudi flung him a glance of pure scorn. "I'm going home now. You're no help at all. Father would do something about these poor people being stoned, but he's out taking the church census today, and he'll be late."

In spite of her fiery words, Trudi lingered. Richard sensed her dread of the empty farmhouse.

"Come on, Trudi. I'll walk over there with you."

"Oh, will you?" A tremulous smile brightened Trudi's face.

Richard took a shortcut across the field Father wanted to buy from the Prince-Bishop. The fresh green of the thin spring grass reminded him of the work everyone in the countryside had started that day—marking the boundary lines between each other's fields.

9

"You're coming to the first-day plowing, aren't you, Trudi?"

Trudi's lips quivered. "I don't know whether I can stand it. All the people around here have homes to go to, but those poor people we saw have been robbed of homes and land. It isn't right. I don't care what the church says." Trudi broke off and clutched Richard's arm. "Look over there—at that bush. There's something moving behind it."

"Probably just a stray goose, Trudi. There are lots of them around."

"Oh, no, it isn't just a goose. It's bigger. Richard, I do believe it's a boy. Look! He's ducked down. He doesn't want us to see him."

Richard glimpsed a boy's cap. "Maybe you're right, Trudi. But why is he playing such a silly game by himself?"

"Haven't you any sense at all? He's one of those Anabaptists. He's escaped. I just know it. Let's see what he does."

They watched for a few minutes. The runaway boy wriggled from clump to clump and headed toward the trees at the edge of the Prince-Bishop's field.

Trudi gasped. "He's going straight into the Prince-Bishop's woods."

"Oh, he can't do that," Richard exclaimed. "No one is allowed in there. He—" Richard checked himself. He must not let himself feel sympathy for an Anabaptist, even a boy his own age. Why should it matter to him what happened to the boy—an outcast of the church? Yet he had to admit to himself that he wanted the boy to escape.

Trudi pulled at his arm. "Richard, do something. The Prince-Bishop might be hunting in there. If he found that poor boy, he would put him in the dungeon."

Paralyzed by his own mixed feelings, Richard did not stir, but the runaway boy's scuttling movements released a flood of pity in him. "Stop," he shouted. "Don't go in there."

The other boy made a startled leap and plunged into the thickest part of the woods.

Trudi moaned in disappointment. "He was too far away. You just scared him."

Richard did not answer. For an instant he had an eerie feeling that he was the other boy, running for his life. "He's gone, Trudi. There's nothing we can do now."

Trudi folded her arms. "Oh, yes, we can. That boy will need food. Tomorrow you and I will take him something to eat."

Richard whirled and faced her. "But no one can go into the Prince-Bishop's woods. It's forbidden. What are you thinking of?"

"Richard Janssen, if you're scared to help a boy in trouble, all alone, frightened, and hungry, just say so."

"I'm not exactly scared, but—" Richard stopped. He could never admit his fear to a girl.

"If you won't go with me, I'll go alone. Do you want that boy to go hungry?"

"No, but—" Richard floundered for words. Trudi's scorn bothered him. She knew as well as he that they should not help the boy. First of all, he was a runaway. That was bad enough. Furthermore, the Prince-Bishop threatened imprisonment to anyone caught trespassing in his private woods. Everyone knew that. But to top it all, the boy was an Anabaptist. Couldn't Trudi understand the danger?

"Richard, it's time you thought about someone besides yourself," Trudi said.

Her tart remark stung him. He followed her to the Schwartz' farmhouse in silence.

"I'm all right now, Richard," Trudi said. "Thank you for coming with me. And remember about tomorrow. Don't you dare tell anyone. It'll be our secret. Promise?"

Richard nodded and started home, confused, yet excited about the next day's adventure. What an odd girl Trudi was—afraid of an empty house, but not afraid to speak her mind, and certainly not afraid of trespassing on the Prince-Bishop's private woods, nor of the Anabaptist runaway. But Anabaptists meant trouble—terrible trouble for anyone caught helping them. Why had he promised to help?

At supper Mother's good broth had somehow lost its flavor. Richard did not dare mention the stoning. Had his parents seen it? He wasn't sure. He kept thinking of the runaway boy. What had happened to him?

Mother had not touched her broth. "Thor, I've been thinking. The land is so poor and the crops won't be any better this year. Why don't you accept your brother's offer?"

Father lowered his spoon. "Go to Münster? But Berthe, you know I'll be buying more land from the Prince-Bishop soon. Besides, we've made more money off our last year's crop than anyone in the parish."

"You're a good carpenter, Thor. There'd be

plenty of work for both of you in your brother's shop."

Richard listened in excitement. "Then I could be with cousin Otto every day," he exclaimed. "I'd like that. Living right over the market square—Oh, Father, let's move to Münster."

Father started to reply, but a heavy pounding at the door interrupted him. The unexpected sound terrified Richard.

"Mr. Janssen!" a man called.

When Father unbolted the door, chilled evening air swept into the room like a nameless, frightening intruder. A sturdy, square-set man with a big book under one arm pushed his way in. It was Hugo Schwartz, Trudi's father. As church census taker, he kept a record of everyone's sins, penances, and punishments. Hidden threats lurked in his deep-set, darting eyes. Richard wondered if Mr. Schwartz really saw people—or was it only their sins?

"You are ready for the census, Mr. Janssen?" A disagreeable rasp in Mr. Schwartz' voice made even innocent words sound sinister.

Mother gasped. "A church census at this time of day?"

"I was delayed by important business this afternoon. Church business." Mr. Schwartz sat down and opened the big book.

Richard stifled a sigh. A church census always took a long time.

"You are the Janssen family—Thor, Berthe, and son Richard?"

"Yes," Father answered.

"You attend the Church of St. Mauritz?"

"Yes."

Richard listened with growing impatience. The familiar questions had never seemed so tiresome. His appetite came back with a rush. The broth looked delicious.

Hugo Schwartz tapped the record book. "I see that Richard was baptized at the cathedral in Münster. Why wasn't he taken to the Church of St. Mauritz? It's closer."

The question startled Richard. Mr. Schwartz had never probed this way before.

Father answered without hesitation. "My brother and his wife live in Münster. Their boy is a few months older than Richard. We wanted them baptized together."

"What is your brother's name?"

"Sigmund Janssen."

"Occupation?"

"Carpenter."

"Children?"

"Just one—Otto."

"Does the family attend mass regularly?"

"Of course. That is, as far as I know. I mean—"

Mr. Schwartz scowled. "Just what do you mean, Mr. Janssen?"

The unspoken threat worried Richard. Did Mr. Schwartz want to make something wrong out of innocent words?

Father answered in his quiet way. "We haven't seen them for some time. There was so much sickness this winter and—"

Mr. Schwartz cut him short. "Have any of you missed services at the Church of St. Mauritz?"

"No."

For the first time since the unexpected knock on the door, Richard relaxed. Who could criticize a perfect record of church attendance?

"Be sure to keep it so." Mr. Schwartz leaned forward. "Excommunication has come to those who transgress."

Richard whispered to himself the word dreaded by every Catholic—excommunication. Those who did not follow the dictates of the church would lose God's mercy forever, even after death.

Mr. Schwartz stood up, but he was not through. "Have you heard any who speak against the church?

"No, I have not."

"Do you know any who belong to that sect everywhere spoken against?"

"Do you mean the ones who baptize twice?" Father asked.

"Precisely. The Anabaptists." Mr. Schwartz spit out the name.

"No, I do not know anyone of that belief," Father said.

"You understand that it is the duty of everyone to seize and deliver to the law those who are rebaptized?"

"Yes, yes, we understand."

Father's impatience nettled Mr. Schwartz. "And you further understand that anyone who gives food or lodging to Anabaptists is liable to heresy and excommunication?"

"Yes, of course, but we do not know such people."

After Mr. Schwartz left, Mother burst out, "What is all this coming to? Why must everyone's loyalty to the church be questioned over and over? It makes me feel guilty even when I'm not."

Father cupped her two hands in his. "Berthe, these are troubled times. We know that people who seemed loyal have turned Anabaptist, but remember, the church protects the faithful."

Richard sighed with relief. The cold broth tasted good.

That night after Richard went to bed, someone outside called his name.

"Richard! Let me in. It's Otto. Wake up, Richard!"

Richard shook himself awake. What was his cousin Otto doing here in the middle of the night? Had something happened to Uncle Sigmund and Aunt Frieda? He hurried down the steep, narrow stairway and unbolted the door. His cousin Otto, a head taller than he, stood outside. Even in the moonlight Richard could see a big lump on Otto's head. Dried blood caked his cap.

"Why, Otto, you're hurt. Whatever has happened?"

"I can't explain now. But I'm hungry, and my head hurts."

A terrible suspicion forced its way into Richard's mind. "Otto, you must tell me something. Did you—were you—" Richard's voice sank to an agonized whisper. "Otto, were you stoned out of Münster this afternoon?"

The look on Otto's face answered him.

Chills of horror and disbelief pounded through Richard's body. Now he had to make a decision. To let an Anabaptist into the house would bring punishment on the whole family. But Otto was hungry and wounded. Should he—could he—turn his own cousin away? What was the right decision?

2

FORBIDDEN TO BELIEVE

THE question pounded over and over in Richard's mind. Did he dare let his cousin Otto, a runaway Anabaptist, into the house? No, he could not take the risk. He turned away from Otto's pleading eyes. Otto slumped against the side of the house.

"I don't blame you for not letting me in, Richard. It's too dangerous for all of you. But could you let me have something to eat? Then I'll go."

His cousin's humble tone and helplessness touched off a sudden, burning resolve in Richard. A surge of reckless daring overcame his first decision. "Otto, I don't care what happens. Come on inside."

He led Otto to the fireplace and fed the embers until a blazing fire warmed the room. He sponged Otto's bruises and brought out bread and cheese. With an effort he kept back the questions he burned to ask and watched Otto eat.

Later, Otto stretched out before the fire. "I never tasted such good food in all my life." His

17

satisfied sigh turned into a yawn. "I'll go before Uncle Thor and Aunt Berthe get up."

"Go where, Otto, and why?"

For a moment Otto did not answer. "It's too long a story to even begin," he said at last.

"But Otto, what happened to your mother and father? Where will they go now? Why didn't you stay with the others? How did you get mixed up with Anabaptists in the first place?" The questions tumbled out.

Otto shook his head. "I'd better go. I don't want to get Uncle Thor and Aunt Berthe into trouble," he said in a stubborn voice, yet he drooped with fatigue.

Richard tried to think what to do. What was it Trudi had said? *It's time you thought about someone besides yourself.* Richard winced at the memory and committed himself to another decision. "You'll go right upstairs to my bed. Don't make any noise. Tomorrow we can decide what to do."

Otto did not protest and fell asleep before Richard pulled the bedcovers over him. But Richard could not sleep. Had he done the right thing? What was he going to tell Mother and Father? That Otto had run away? That he had been stoned out of Münster? That he would have to be turned over to the church authorities?

18   When Richard went downstairs the next morning, the questions were still unanswered. Someone knocked at the door. Richard's heart thudded. Had someone seen Otto come to the Janssen house? Or had Trudi's overzealous father somehow wormed information from her about the runaway she had seen? What if Mr. Schwartz had already reported to the church authorities?

Richard waited in nervous torment until Father unbolted the door. The next moment Aunt Frieda staggered into the house. Uncle Sigmund limped behind her. Aunt Frieda hugged a tiny bundle to her heart. With set, pale face she gazed around, her blue eyes unblinking.

Mother helped Aunt Frieda to a bench near the fireplace and then gasped, "Why, Frieda Janssen, it's a baby. Why didn't you let us know?"

Tears started in Aunt Frieda's eyes. "He's sick. We had to come. We had no other place to go."

"Why, of course." Mother sounded as if dawn visitors were not a bit unusual. "But where's Otto?"

Aunt Frieda and Uncle Sigmund exchanged glances. Uncle Sigmund shook his head and pursed his lips in warning.

"I'm sure he can take care of himself with God's help," Aunt Frieda said. "But the baby is sick. I've been so worried."

She undid a flap of cloth and raised up the tiny baby. Richard stared at his new cousin. This creature with tiny puckered lips and wrinkled forehead seemed like a stranger in the midst of faces he knew so well.

Mother took the baby. Her face lit up with smiles. Richard watched her in astonishment. Mother had never seemed so young and pretty.

"He's beautiful. He doesn't look sick now, but I'm so glad you came here." Mother made a bed for the baby in a large, oval market basket. "What are you going to name him?"

"His name is Karl Josef," Aunt Frieda said.

Mother clucked her disappointment. "Then he's already baptized?"

"No."

Mother brightened at once. "May we help with the christening?"

Father chimed in. "We'll have a real christening feast. I've got a good green cheese aging, and we'll invite all the neighbors." He warmed up to the idea. "Why, we'll have a celebration as big as the one when Richard and Otto were baptized."

Uncle Sigmund cleared his throat. "We're sorry, but that will be impossible. You see, we are moving to Strasbourg now."

"But why?" Mother and Father asked.

Richard felt his parents' shock and disapproval, yet he sympathized with his aunt and uncle bowed under their terrible burden.

Uncle Sigmund sighed. "It's better not to explain."

Father stirred the fire so hard that the sparks flew. "You have a good business in Münster," he said. Richard sensed his father's effort to remain calm. "You're not just a master carpenter. You're an artist. Don't people like carved furniture anymore?"

Father's attempt at joking brought no response. Uncle Sigmund and Aunt Frieda sat staring at the floor. Richard wanted to soothe them, to say that everything would be all right, that God would take care of them. Then the thought struck him like the blow of a hammer. Which God—Catholic or Anabaptist? Or was there one God for both? The question haunted him.

"But at least you can wait for the christening," Father was saying. "We have plenty of room here."

Aunt Frieda bent over the baby. Without looking up, she said in a low voice, "There isn't going to be a christening here or anywhere else."

Father jumped up. "What's this she's saying, Sigmund? Refusing to have a Janssen baby christened? You have to give the baby a name, and you have to baptize him in the church. Now, what is all this foolishness about not having a christening?"

Uncle Sigmund's earnest face paled. "You see, Thor, our beliefs have changed. We feel that no child should be baptized until he is old enough himself to choose Christ as his Saviour. We believe that no one else has the right to do it for him."

Father's mouth sagged open. "But the church

forbids such belief. Do you realize this is heresy? Have you considered the consequences? You're not only putting an innocent baby's soul in jeopardy, you are inviting excommunication, persecution, even death for yourselves."

"We know."

"Don't you remember what happened in Münster only six years ago?"

"Yes."

"Are you telling us you belong to that sect everywhere spoken against?" Father forced out the words between clenched teeth.

Uncle Sigmund rose and faced the family. "We call ourselves the Brethren. Others in derision call us Anabaptists."

The word *Anabaptists* uncoiled around the little room like a deadly snake.

Mother put her hands to her lips. Her face showed both terror and concern.

"As for persecution," Uncle Sigmund went on, "we have tasted that already."

"You—you mean the stoning?" Mother whispered. "Were you with *them*?"

"Yes."

"But the baby was sick," Aunt Frieda put in. "We hid until dark and came back here to get help."

The baby began to cry. While the whole family hovered over it, Richard ran upstairs and told Otto the news.

"You'll have to go downstairs now," he said.

"I won't. I'm not going to Strasbourg, no matter what anybody says."

"But aren't you one of them?"

"One of them what?"

"You know what I mean," Richard said.

"How can I know? You'll have to say what you mean." Otto rolled over in bed and rubbed his eyes.

"Well, then, are you an Ana—Anabaptist?"

"No. You have to be baptized again to be an Anabaptist."

Richard shivered. "That would be a terrible sin. I don't blame you for being afraid."

"I don't think it's a sin, and I'm not afraid." Otto stood up. "My parents said I could choose for myself. They say I have to experience God's Spirit within me before I can be an Anabaptist. I don't exactly know what kind of experience that is, and I'm going to wait until I'm sure."

"Then you're still a Catholic?"

Otto thumped the pillow. "I suppose so. One thing I do know is that I'm not going to Strasbourg."

"Why are your parents going?"

"Because there's an Anabaptist leader there, that's why. His name is Melchior Hofmann, and he's in prison. But I don't care about that. I want to stay in Münster. Our rooms overlook the square. You can see everything—people setting up their stalls on market days. There's always something exciting going on." Otto thumped the pillow again.

Richard sat on the edge of the bed. "But you can't live there alone." He thought a moment. "Why don't you ask your parents if you can stay with me? Then you wouldn't have to go to Strasbourg. We could go to school together."

Otto gave a little jump. All his listlessness disappeared. "Say, I'd like that."

"Then go on downstairs and talk it over," Richard said. "I have to take the cows to pasture."

On his way through the kitchen Richard heard a tap at the back door. It was so quiet, so cautious, that at first he thought it must be a goose sidling too close to the house. But the tap came again, secret, almost pleading. Richard opened the door the width of his hand. Trudi stood outside with a basket covered with a snowy white cloth.

"I've got to talk to you, Richard," she whispered. "Don't tell anyone I'm here. It's very important."

Richard stepped outside and shut the door behind him. "I've got something to tell you, too, Trudi." He grinned in anticipation. His news would top anything Trudi had to say.

She did not wait for him. "I can't go with you to take food to that boy."

"But—"

"Don't interrupt. I have to hurry right back. Father mustn't find out I've left the house." She glanced over her shoulder. "You see, I found out something awful about my father—" Tears welled up in her eyes. "Oh, Richard, my own father was one of the men who stoned those poor people. He hates them. You should have heard him shout and rave." She shuddered. "It was terrible. He vows to run them all out of the country. What are we going to do?"

Richard gulped down his shock and fear. Trudi's news brought danger to the very doorstep of the Janssen family. If Mr. Schwartz even suspected that Otto and his parents were in the house, Richard knew only too well what would happen next. Not only Otto and his parents would be stoned out of the parish for the second time, but Father and Mother, too. Already Richard could feel the impact of stones thrown in hatred, could hear the terrifying shouts of maddened men.

He longed to tell Trudi about Otto, but he could not do so now. Mr. Schwartz' violent temper would erupt on Trudi if he ever found out her sympathy for an Anabaptist.

"But you'll find the boy, won't you?" Trudi was pleading. "I've worried about him out there all night. He's cold and hungry." She thrust the basket into Richard's hands. "Here's food. Father made me promise to tell him if I ever see any strangers. Oh, he's so violent I'm afraid of him. So when you do go and find that boy, don't even tell me about it. That way I won't have to lie to Father. You do understand, don't you?"

"Of course, Trudi." Why had he worried so much? Everything was working out better than he had hoped. Then to his horror he heard Otto call out, "Richard, where are you? They've agreed! I can stay."

Otto came out. Richard sagged down on the bench by the back door. Now Trudi would have to tell her father about this stranger. Richard choked out an introduction. "Trudi, this is my cousin Otto."

At first Trudi looked startled, then flashed a smile of recognition. "Why, I remember you from last year—at the harvest festival." Without waiting for an answer, she added, "I suppose you've come for the spring plowing?"

Otto flushed and stammered, "Not exactly. I mean, it sounds like a good idea."

Richard tingled with relief. *Trudi did not connect Otto with the runaway boy.* Otto was safe.

A hoarse, angry shout resounded over the field. Trudi paled. "That's Father. I must go back."

"Trudi!" There was no mistaking the anger in Mr. Schwartz' raspy voice.

Otto grabbed Richard's arm. "That's one of them—one of the men yesterday. I'd recognize his voice any place."

Richard squeezed Otto's hand in warning, but he was too late. A horrified understanding was written on Trudi's face. She stared at Otto.

"Then you're not just visiting here?" For the first time she seemed to notice Otto's bruised face. "You're the boy who ran away."

Her slow, measured tones sounded to Richard like the parish church bell tolling a death.

Otto tried to grin. "Yes," he said, but the word hung in the air like a question.

In silent appeal, Richard studied Trudi's expression. *What are you going to do, Trudi? Are you going to tell your father about Otto?*

In Trudi's eyes he read the same conflict that had tortured him the night before when Otto came. What decision would Trudi make?

26

3

PREACHER WITHOUT A PULPIT

RICHARD knew that everything depended on Trudi's decision. He fought down an impulse to run.

Trudi stared first at Richard, then at Otto. "You two look enough alike to be brothers." Her eyes began to sparkle with excitement. "If Father doesn't see you together, he'd never have to find out that Otto was staying here."

"Otto!" Uncle Sigmund called from the front room. "What are you doing? Come back in. We have a lot to talk over."

"That doesn't sound like your father, Richard," Trudi said in alarm.

Richard groaned. "No, that's Uncle Sigmund. He and Aunt Frieda are here—and the baby," he added. "They were stoned out of Münster yesterday."

Trudi's shoulders slumped. "But this is terrible! What can we possibly do now?" Then she straightened. "Otto, go in and tell them to hide." Her voice was crisp with decision. "Hurry!

Tell them Father's a fanatic. He'll go to any lengths to get rid of the Anabaptists." She pushed at Otto with impatient hands.

"Wait a minute, Trudi." Otto sounded calm. "Let Richard go instead. Let's find out whether your father will mistake me for Richard." He prodded Richard into the house. "There's no time to argue. Here he comes."

Richard shut the door behind him, raced inside to warn the others, and came back to listen to Trudi's father.

Mr. Schwartz stormed into the backyard. "What are you doing here, Trudi? Mrs. Walther came over to tell me the new pastor's coming to visit. Get back to the house at once."

"Yes, Father."

"As for you, Richard, why aren't you out with the cattle?"

"Uh—Father needed me," Otto said. "He's inside."

Richard heard Mr. Schwartz grunt. In a few moments Otto opened the door. A grin spread across his face. "It worked. He thinks I'm you."

In high spirits, the boys pounded each other on the back and relived the incident in every detail. Then a high, piercing voice sounded outside. "Mrs. Janssen, let me in."

Richard recognized the voice of the fat, bustling parish gossip, Mrs. Walther. Why was she making the rounds this morning? Had she seen something unusual going on? He ran to warn the others. "It's Mrs. Walther."

Mother sprang to her feet with a gasp. "She mustn't see who's here, and above all, she mustn't see the baby. The news would be all over the parish in no time."

Father opened the door to the stairs. "Sigmund, you and Frieda take the baby and go upstairs. You, too, Otto. I'm going to the fields out the back way. No use giving the old gossip anything more to wonder about."

"What about me?" Richard asked.

"You stay here behind the door where you can see and hear everything that goes on. If anything happens, come and get me. But if we can keep people from finding out anyone else is here, so much the better. We can decide later what to do."

Father hurried out. Richard settled himself at the bottom of the stairs, inching the door open enough so that he could see through the crack.

Mrs. Walther puffed and blew her way into the house, removed her short, dark blue cape and settled in Father's favorite chair.

"Have you see the new pastor yet? I thought he might stop here first before going to Mr. Schwartz' house. I was talking to Mr. Schwartz just a little while ago. My, what a zealous Christian he is. What a service he is doing for the church tracking down those Anabaptist traitors. I am sure the new pastor will be just as zealous." Mrs. Walther folded her fat arms across her ample chest and beamed at Mother. "I understand some of those runaway Anabaptists are hiding in the neighborhood."

Mother's reply was indistinct.

Mrs. Walther moved her head from side to side like a hungry cow nibbling at thin grass. "You know about the committee, don't you?" She did not wait for an answer. "Mr. Schwartz thought of it all by himself. My husband is on it, and yours will be, of course. The committee have pledged themselves to rid the parish of all Anabaptists."

Richard watched and listened with growing impatience. Did Mrs. Walther know about Uncle Sigmund's family being stoned yesterday, or didn't she? Was she playing a cat-and-mouse game? Or was she just talking?

Mrs. Walther continued. "Mr. Schwartz' committee is doing fine work. They've run a lot of people out of Münster already. Some of them are going to Strasbourg. There's a big group of Anabaptists there—at least two thousand." Mrs. Walther rocked with the rhythm of her words. "My, aren't these terrible times?"

Mother murmured some response that Richard could not hear.

A baby's cry from upstairs stopped Mrs. Walther midway in her rocking. "Why, that's a baby. Is that why Trudi came over here this morning?"

Mother sighed but did not say anything.

Mrs. Walther waited, then rushed on. "I love babies. I didn't realize you'd had one. It isn't baptized yet, is it? Why don't you have it done at the cathedral in Münster? It's a lovely place. I always have our stall as close to it as possible on market days so I can step inside for spiritual refreshment." She closed her eyes and let her head drop forward for a moment. Then she jerked forward. "Perhaps you are planning to let the new pastor baptize it?"

"No, not exactly—" Mother stammered. "I mean—"

Richard twisted in sympathy. Mother couldn't lie, he knew. Was she going to tell too much?

Mrs. Walther rattled on. "Why don't you take it to church tomorrow and have it baptized? You can't be too careful these times. The Anabaptists might snatch up a baby and never let him be baptized until he's eleven or twelve. Can you imagine such a devilish belief?"

While Mrs. Walther talked, Richard tried to think of some way to get her out of the house. Every minute she stayed meant danger to the entire family. But Mrs. Walther looked prepared to stay forever.

"The way these Anabaptists are taking hold, first thing you know, an Anabaptist might move right here into this neighborhood. How would you like to have an Anabaptist next door— or have your boy there marry an Anabaptist when he grows up? Doesn't the thought terrify you?"

"Mrs. Walther, people should be able to live in peace with each other whatever their beliefs," Mother said. "You must admit the Anabaptists have the courage to suffer for their convictions."

"Why, Mrs. Janssen! I never thought I'd hear such talk from you!" Mrs. Walther struggled out of the chair, her cheeks red. She backed toward the door as if she thought Mother would attack her. "I must be going."

"I'm sorry your errand was fruitless," Mother said.

"Oh, I think it was worth my while." With a meaningful glance toward the stairway, Mrs. Walther left.

Later, when the family was together, Uncle Sigmund talked of leaving at once. Otto could stay with Richard, and if he kept out of Mr. Schwartz' way, there was no reason why the two boys could not attend the new pastor's school. Yet somehow day after day passed and his relatives did not leave.

Richard noticed that while Uncle Sigmund stayed hidden during the day, he and Father went out for walks at twilight. Richard itched to know where they went and what they talked about. He hated to say anything to Otto. Somehow his cousin fended off any discussion about his parents. Richard became more and more curious about Anabaptist beliefs.

Mother and Aunt Frieda had long conversations in the house. Both talked in low voices.

Once, when he found Aunt Frieda alone, Richard blurted out a question long on his mind. "Aren't you afraid all the time, being an Anabaptist?"

Aunt Frieda's face softened. "I may show outward, human fear, but once you know the true presence of Christ within, you can stand anything." Her blue eyes shone with earnestness. "We are not going to invite persecution on purpose, but if we have to suffer for the sake of the truth we believe, God will give us the strength to bear all for His sake."

Richard thought about what Aunt Frieda said. It really took courage to be an Anabaptist and believe in principles that no one else did. He felt that Mother and Father had begun to respect Uncle Sigmund's and Aunt Frieda's beliefs, but when Sunday came, he saw how different it was to be an Anabaptist. His relatives could not go to church anymore. Otto, although not an Anabaptist, could not go either. There would be too many questions. People would see how much he and Otto resembled each other, and they would remember.

On this Sunday, even at a distance, Richard saw that something unusual was happening. People crowded in the churchyard. Why weren't they going in? Instead, they gathered in clusters. Women bent their tightly capped heads and whispered behind their hands. Men stood with feet apart, shaking their heads. Often, all spoke at once.

The talk flowed on all sides.

"Have you heard about the new pastor?" the parish miller asked.

"I've heard he's an outspoken, God-fearing man," someone said.

"He's going to overthrow the church."

"What! Impossible."

"But it's true. I heard it from Mr. Schwartz himself."

Several people murmured their disapproval.

"I understand he has very strong views," the parish blacksmith said.

Several other men hummed a question.

"But he's sincere."

"Oh, yes, very sincere," Mr. Walther said in mockery. "All the heretics are sincere. Even Anabaptists are sincere, you know, but the church calls it heresy."

"Hush," someone warned. "Don't talk about Anabaptists."

From time to time people turned to gaze at the church doors.

Richard saw that the doors were nailed shut. Wooden bars ran the full width of the ornate doors. In the center panel a square of white paper fluttered from a nail.

A man ran up to look at the sign, then backed off and scratched his head.

"What does it say?" Mrs. Walther bellowed.

"I don't know. I can't read."

"Who can?" Mrs. Walther wanted to know. "There must be someone who can. Where are those boys the other pastor taught to read?" She lunged forward and pointed to Richard. "Go up there and read it."

Richard made his way to the door, stood on tiptoe and read aloud,

"'Notice: All persons are to take heed that by order of the town council the doors of this church are shut and that they are prohibited from holding any meetings therein, or to open the doors without license from authority until further orders, as they will answer the contrary to their peril.'"

Everyone exclaimed in fright and shock.

Mr. Schwartz shoved his way forward. "Yes, yes, this is all true. I know all about it. Haven't you people heard the latest news?"

"No, Mr. Schwartz." Mrs. Walther wedged her plump form in the front line of bystanders. "What's happened? Is the new pastor ill?"

"Worse than that."

A gasp rose from every throat.

"Is he dead?" someone whispered.

Mr. Schwartz waved his short arms until a

34

hush settled over the crowd. "He has been forbidden to preach."

Someone exhaled in almost a sob. "Then that's why the doors are locked."

At once the people craned their necks to look, as if somehow they could stare the doors open.

"What's to become of us?" Mrs. Walther wailed. Her large frame shook with sobs. "Our shepherd taken away. What will become of his sheep?" She burst into noisy weeping.

At this moment fresh exclamations rose. "But there he is!"

The new pastor, in his priest's robes, pressed through the crowd. Cheer upon cheer burst out.

"Open the doors, Pastor!" someone called.

But the pastor did not turn toward the church. Tall and handsome, he looked over the congregation with a slight smile. Mr. Schwartz roared with anger, but was quickly hushed by the people nearest him.

"Friends," the pastor began.

The congregation quieted.

"I have come today to tell you about the true religion. It is first of all faith in Christ and the practice of brotherly love. I have just returned from Friesland, and there I received new truth from a man called Menno Simons—"

He was not allowed to finish. A group of soldiers holding iron-tipped pikes plunged through the people and grasped his arms.

"You are forbidden to preach, Pastor," the leader said. "You will come with us."

The soldiers clamped their hands on the pastor's shoulders and pushed him ahead. Amid the sobs and murmurs of the congregation, the armed men jostled the priest toward the road.

The new pastor twisted in their grasp and shouted to the stunned spectators, "Do not be dismayed at what you see. God alone can close my lips."

As soon as the pastor had been led away, Hugh Schwartz took charge again. "Our leader has betrayed us, but for your protection there is a special committee who is ridding the countryside of the heretical sect called Anabaptists."

An undercurrent of hissing at the word "committee" almost silenced Mr. Schwartz. He began to shout. "Anabaptists are being sheltered by the disloyal and unfaithful. They have unauthorized meetings in secret places. Those of you who have guilty knowledge of such actions, be warned. The church punishes transgressors."

Mr. Schwartz' words pierced Richard like a bitter wind. Who gave Mr. Schwartz the right to speak for the church? Was the church supposed to tell people what to think? In his heart he knew the answer. People were supposed to do their own thinking, guided by God's Word.

Mr. Schwartz strutted back and forth. "Now, good people, go home. Let all traitors in the parish know that their hour has come. The committee will flush them out of every hiding place, from every cellar, from every attic. I say unto you, woe to those who try to hide these heretics—and their children. Be warned, for you know not at what hour the committee will come to every house in the parish."

How long would Uncle Sigmund, Aunt Frieda, and his cousins be safe? What if the committee arrived at the house before he could warn them?

Panic-stricken at the thought, Richard started to run.

4

THE MEETING PLACE

ON the way home Richard looked back several times, half expecting to see the committee at his heels ready to start their cellar-to-attic search. How long would it take them to visit every house in the parish? How many other people were hiding Anabaptist relatives or friends?

Uncle Sigmund shrugged away Richard's warning and talked with intense enthusiasm. "You see, all over Germany the brethren are springing up in independent groups. Don't you see what this means? The living truth of the Bible has begun to enter in the hearts of men. You do feel that the Bible was meant to be in everyone's hands, not just the priests', don't you?" he asked Father.

"Yes, I've always felt that," Father said.

"Then did you believe that the church was right when it tried to prevent the Bible from being translated into German?"

Father looked thoughtful. "I must confess that restriction never seemed right to me."

"You do have a Bible, don't you?" Uncle Sigmund asked.

"Yes." Father upended a stool covered with a ruffle. On the underside a Bible hung suspended in a sling.

Uncle Sigmund laughed. "You see? God's truth is working on you like a seed sprouting in the ground. Open your heart to His influence. Tell me one thing, though. Will you turn us over to the committee when they come?"

Father buried his face in his hands. "You know I could not turn you in—although I know it is wrong to keep you here. I don't know what to do."

A choking helplessness tormented Richard. What could anyone do?

"There is always one never-failing source of strength," Uncle Sigmund said. "Let us pray for guidance."

In his heart Richard knew Uncle Sigmund had given the right answer. Who but God could help them now?

The two men prayed in turn until the room vibrated with their earnest entreaties.

In a little while Father burst out, "The only message I feel is that we are a family, and we must stick together. I do not know where all this is leading, but I will be responsible for my actions, whatever happens."

Uncle Sigmund smiled. "God will guide you and give you strength. You'll see. As for the brethren, He will lead us out of danger, if that is His will, and if we are to suffer for His sake, He will give us strength to endure. Let us not be frightened though the hounds bay and the lions roar. God who is with us is a mighty God and will keep His own."

Richard kept remembering Uncle Sigmund's words throughout the long afternoon. He and Otto looked down the road every few minutes, but no one came to the house. The next day Father and Uncle Sigmund left early. Richard and Otto took turns as lookouts. When at last Richard spotted several men approaching, he felt almost relieved. He recognized one of the men—Mr. Walther, husband of the parish gossip. He ran inside.

"They're coming."

Mother's lips clamped shut with determination. She glanced at the back door and the stairway. Richard knew the thought in everyone's mind. *Hide the baby.*

"But where?" Aunt Frieda asked as if the thought had been spoken.

In the desperate silence, a strange idea came to Richard. "Like Moses," he said. His own words astonished him. Where had the idea come from?

The others stared at him.

"We could hide Karl Josef like Moses outdoors in the bushes," Richard rushed on. "He's already in a market basket."

"Yes, of course. That's the answer. And, thank God, he's asleep." Mother helped Aunt Frieda cover the baby.

"I'll hide him outside." Otto hurried out with the basket.

Aunt Frieda ran upstairs, and Richard hid in the stairwell behind the door and peeked through the crack. The men clumped into the house. Mr. Walther, a thin-faced man, led the group.

"What brings you here?" Mother asked.

40

"We're just getting a few facts ready for the next church census," Mr. Walther said in a high whine. "I understand you have an unbaptized baby in the house."

"What makes you think that?" Mother asked. "Did someone tell you that just to make trouble for us? Isn't my husband well respected in this parish? Is there anything in the census that shows we are disloyal to the church? A false accusation could mean trouble for you and these other men."

Mr. Walther coughed. "We just thought the baby might belong to your relatives from Münster."

Richard heard Mother force a laugh. "Is there a baby on the record books?"

After a moment's pause, Mr. Walther said, "Well, no, but there are rumors about this baby. Perhaps it was all a mistake."

"My husband will be home soon, and I don't know what he will think about your coming," Mother said. "Do you wish to wait for him?"

"Oh no, of course not. We all respect Mr. Janssen," Mr. Walther spoke a little too fast. Richard smiled. Father was not easily angered, but if necessary, he could overpower any man in the parish.

"But I understand your position, Mr. Walther. In these days, with Anabaptists still rising up against the church, you can't be too careful." 41

"Yes, that's it. That's it exactly. Thank you, Mrs. Janssen."

The men shuffled out.

Otto brought in the market basket. When Aunt Frieda came downstairs, she wept with relief. "He slept through it all! What a miracle. It was God's hand," she said.

"All we needed was bulrushes for our Moses," Otto laughed.

In the good-natured teasing that followed, Richard asked himself how he happened to think of Moses at just the right moment to save Karl Josef from being discovered and seized for baptism. The answer came in a flash of insight. It was God, of course, working within, like a still, small voice. For an instant, he understood why people risked their lives to keep a close personal contact with God.

In the days that followed, the two families talked and talked, read the Bible, and prayed together. Sometimes the grown-ups lowered their voices when Richard came near. What were they planning? An air of secrecy pervaded the whole house.

One day Richard could stand it no longer. He took Otto outside. "Everybody has secrets around here."

Otto nodded. "That's the way it was in Münster, too. My father and some other men used to go someplace and come back all dirty. He never talked about it when I was around. I've wondered and wondered where they went. It had something to do with the Anabaptists, of course."

"How did the committee find out about you?"

"I don't know."

"What was it like?" Richard persisted, his mind on the stoning.

"What was what like?"

"Being stoned."

"It hurt." Otto touched the bruise on his head.

"Weren't you afraid?"

"Oh, after it began, it wasn't too bad." Otto sounded almost smug.

"I don't think I'd be that brave," Richard said.

"Well, you were brave when you let me in the other night. You don't have to fight to be brave."

"I guess that's true. I should have thought of that myself."

Otto burst out, "We have to be brave whether we want to be or not. If it isn't the committee that tracks down Anabaptists, it'll be the *Rat* in Münster—."

"What is the *Rat*?"

"The city council. I used to watch all of them go into the town hall to have their meetings. Anyhow, they aren't the only ones who can go after the Anabaptists. The Prince-Bishop's soldiers can do anything he wants them to, and he's over everybody, even the *Rat*. His soldiers can kill people. All they have to say is that it's in the name of the church."

A nameless dread cut into Richard's bones. What could anybody do in the face of such enemies? Who would protect them? Who but God? But which side would He take?

"Otto, how long do you think it will be before the committee here finds out about your parents?"

"Who can tell that?" Otto shrugged and turned away. "I've been thinking, though—"

"What about? Tell me."

"We ought to make a secret hiding place somewhere." Otto plucked a blade of grass and chewed on it. "Yes, I've been thinking about this for a long time."

"Do you mean a secret hiding place for your folks or for other people, too?"

"For all those who are hounded from their homes, as we were."

Otto's idea aroused Richard's imagination. "You mean someplace where people store food and clothes and help each other escape?"

"Exactly."

"It's a wonderful idea. But where would you find a place to hide?"

Otto grinned again. "How about the Prince-Bishop's woods?"

"But no one's allowed in there."

"All the better. No one would come snooping."

Richard could not suppress his excitement. "Let's go over there—right now. No one will miss us."

Otto needed no urging. The two boys crossed the Prince-Bishop's field. At the edge of the woods, Otto pushed through the underbrush without hesitation. Twigs crackled underfoot. The rustle of small living things made Richard's scalp prickle. All the time he was aware of life about him. It was as if something big and breathing stirred in the dark green depths of the forest, as if something nameless watched the movement of the intruders.

In sudden panic, he hurried to catch up with Otto, who at that moment stopped. Richard tripped and grabbed a shrub to break his fall. The shrub gave way, and Richard bumped into his cousin. Both boys fell onto a mound of freshly turned dirt. They scrambled to their feet.

Richard brushed off his tunic with trembling fingers. "Maybe this isn't such a good idea after all. Don't you think we'd better go back?" He tried to make his voice sound natural.

Otto hissed a reply. "No, not now. There's something going on in here, and I think I know what. Come on."

Richard obeyed. In the next half hour he must have stepped over a hundred half-hidden tree roots.

Without warning, Otto stopped. "I hear something," he whispered.

Richard felt a slight tremor in the underbrush. Otto put his fingers to his lips and threw himself on the ground. Richard crept close by. The thick underbrush near them moved. Richard held his breath until he thought his lungs would burst. Why had Otto ever suggested exploring the Prince-Bishop's woods?

A muffled squeal from the bushes behind him sent shivers down his back. He did not want to turn around and look, but he had to. Two small, dirty hands parted the brush. A flood of regret swept over him for ever coming so far. Otto, too, trembled.

Above them someone exclaimed, "Oh!" Then in a clear voice heightened by excitement, a girl breathed, "Richard Janssen! Otto! What are you doing here flat on the ground?"

It was Trudi Schwartz. Richard jumped up and began to brush the dirt off his clothes. Otto rolled over and sat with his hands clasped around his knees. He grinned at Trudi. "We're probably doing just what you are—exploring."

"What are you doing here, Trudi?" Richard asked.

"Something has been going on here," Trudi said. "For several evenings about twilight I've seen some men and women go into these woods. They come from all directions, and they slip in so secretly I just know there is some kind of secret meeting going on. It isn't the Prince-Bishop's men," she added. "Anyhow, I just had to find out for myself."

"Let's do it together, then," Richard said.

They pushed through thick underbrush until all at once they broke through into a cleared area. Rough-hewn logs had been placed lengthwise on three sides. A narrow but deep stream formed the fourth side.

"What is this supposed to be?" Trudi asked in wonderment.

"It's a church!" Otto's voice rose in excitement. "The Anabaptists have to have a secret church. There must be secret churches like this all over Germany. I've heard my father say there are thousands of Anabaptists now."

"Then all those people were really coming to church," Trudi exclaimed in triumph.

"Not only that, but they can hide here if they are persecuted," Otto said.

Richard puzzled over the bareness of the clearing. "If this is a church, where are the candles and incense and images?"

Otto snorted. "Anabaptists don't have things like that."

Trudi sat down on a fallen log. The afternoon sun filtered golden shafts through the tree branches. "It's so peaceful, somehow. It feels like a church. I like it."

"Well, you won't ever have to hide out here," Richard said.

An odd expression crossed Trudi's face. "No, I suppose not."

Richard could not imagine how the clearing could be a church. "It's so bare. There isn't even a cross. What do people do when they come here?"

As if in answer, he heard a rustling sound in the brush.

Trudi's eyes widened. "Somebody's coming."

"Hide behind these bushes," Otto commanded.

Trudi darted behind the thick shrubs. Richard and Otto followed. All three crouched on hands and knees.

The air became suddenly stifling. A tight band of dread wound around Richard's scalp.

The rustling sounds increased. Were they animal or human? Men's voices murmured not far away. The next minute a man crawled through an underbrush passageway and stood up. Uncle Sigmund! Somehow his being there seemed fitting. The next man crawled through. Richard recognized his father and all but cried out. Now he understood the secrecy and hushed talk of the past few days. Had Father, once the most loyal of Catholics, become an Anabaptist?

5

TOO MANY SECRETS

CHILLED and trembling, Richard sank back on
his heels. If Father had become an Anabaptist,
was Mother one, too?

Trudi looked at Richard, her face tight and
strained. She lost her balance and caught hold of
a shrub to steady herself. To Richard the rustle
of the twigs sounded like thunder. What if Uncle
Sigmund and Father discovered all three of them
spying? Richard nudged Otto. "Let's go," he
whispered. Otto shook his head.

There was nothing to do but watch. Father
knelt on the ground near the stream. Uncle Sigmund placed his hand on Father's shoulder. "Have
you repented of all your sins and forsaken them?"

"Yes."

"Do you wish to be baptized in the name of
Jesus Christ for the remission of sins and for the
gift of the Holy Ghost?"

"I do," Father replied in a firm voice.

In the peaceful green of the woods, Uncle
Sigmund baptized Father. With one hand at

the back of Father's head and his other hand holding Father's clasped hands he said softly, "I now baptize you in the name of the Father, the Son, and the Holy Ghost." Then in a clear voice: "Therefore we are buried with Him by baptism into death: that like as Christ was raised up from the dead by the glory of the Father, even so we also should walk in newness of life."

A strange, tingling joy throbbed in Richard's veins, a living presence that he had never known before. Was this what it would be like to be an Anabaptist? Father knelt with Uncle Sigmund, and both men offered joyful praise to God.

Richard felt he could stay no longer. Otto and Trudi followed him in silence. At the edge of the woods, Richard stopped and looked at the others. "So that's what Anabaptists do."

"Wasn't the baptism beautiful?" Trudi exclaimed. "In the woods everything seems so much closer to God. Didn't you feel something different?"

Otto nodded. "Yes, I did. But I was surprised. I didn't expect to see a baptism, and Uncle Thor, of all people."

"Would you have the courage to be baptized the second time, Otto?" Trudi asked.

"Certainly. Why shouldn't I? One of these days I may surprise everyone—including my- self—" His voice trailed off.

Curiosity stirred Richard. "You—you mean you might be rebaptized?"

"I wouldn't unless I felt sure," Otto said.

"What would you have to be sure of?" Trudi asked.

"Whether God's Spirit was telling me to do

it or whether it was Satan. That's what our priest kept telling us when he talked against the Anabaptists."

"How could you tell which it is?" Trudi probed.

"That I don't know."

"How about you, Richard?" Trudi asked.

Richard echoed the question to himself. How could anyone know? But he knew one thing: It took courage to be an Anabaptist. He blurted, "I'll be baptized whenever Otto is."

Otto cocked his head to one side. "It's not as easy as that. You have to do a lot of thinking first. Nobody likes Anabaptists, and worse things than stoning can happen to you."

At home again, an invisible band of tension tightened around Richard's head. Neither he nor Otto spoke more than they had to. Neither Father nor Uncle Sigmund mentioned the afternoon in the woods. Sometimes Richard thought he must have dreamed the whole scene.

"How long before the committee finds out?" he asked himself in bed that night. "What will happen to all of us then?"

How long? How long? The words sang in his ears.

On the day spring plowing began, Otto insisted on going.

"Everyone will be so busy, no one will have time to notice me," he argued. "Besides, you'll need help, Uncle Thor."

Father hesitated, then agreed, but he would not let Uncle Sigmund come. "You'd better stay in the house and do your wood carving." He pointed to the cradle Uncle Sigmund was making. "We don't want to take any chances."

Spring plowing, like harvesting, was a parish event. Everyone exchanged hopes for good crops and lush grass to pasture the scrawny oxen, lean from the hard winter. They avoided the Prince-Bishop's woods. No one ventured on the Prince-Bishop's field adjoining, even though its sparse green grass looked thicker than the community pastureland.

The crisp biting spring air excited Richard. He and Otto raced along the ridges that lay back to back outlining the land strips belonging to different families. Usually, everyone chattered and laughed at first-day plowing, but this year, people moved with caution.

"Did you hear?" someone asked Father. Without waiting for an answer, the plowman went on. "The Prince-Bishop is hiring more soldiers."

At first Richard did not understand why.

The plowman was eager to explain. "I understand these Anabaptists are getting out of hand again." He laughed slyly. "The Anabaptists are good workers, I hear. That should please the Prince side of the Prince-Bishop well enough. But since the Prince is also the Bishop, it looks like trouble." The plowman checked a quick laugh and explained his joke in detail. "The Prince says to the Anabaptists, 'Give me your rents and tithes,' and the Bishop says, 'No, you can't till these lands. Get out. You're heretics.'" The plowman laughed until tears ran down his cheeks. "And the Prince-Bishop is one and the same man."

Under the spring sun, happy shouts, laughter, and talking drifted over the fields. Women and girls prepared rude trestle tables for the community lunches. The men streamed in, flushed, wiping their foreheads with their three-fingered plowing gloves. They talked, slapped each other on the back, and shouted jokes to each other.

"Hans, here, thought he was an ox," one plowman called out. "He got so excited, he pulled the plow by himself. He thought the oxen were hitched up, and they weren't. He plowed a half meter before he found out the oxen still stood under a tree."

There was a burst of laughter. "So Hans is an ox," people teased.

"Well, I wanted to get through this strip so that mine would be plowed next." Hans blushed and dug his fingers into his rough neckband.

For days men helped each other plow the land strips. Several people would team up their thin oxen and plow first on one strip and then on another.

At last the day came when it was Father's turn to have the oxen and his neighbors to help. One man came up coughing in embarrassment. "I wish I could help today, Mr. Janssen, but my wife is home very ill, and I must mind the children until she gets on her feet again, God willing that she do so."

"That's quite all right," Father said. "There are so many to help."

Another plowman sidled up, looked at the ground, and scraped one leg with his foot. "I beg to be excused," he said, "but I fell off old Fritz, my second horse, and it's like someone had tied my back into a knot. I do regret that I can't help with your plowing."

Father looked a bit puzzled. "Of course, of course. I quite understand, and be careful of that back."

Was this a warning of some kind? Richard could not help but wonder.

A third man came up. "Something has overcome my geese—must be bewitched, I guess, but I will have to stay home to take care of them or I'll lose them all, and a poor man nowadays can't take a risk like that. So if you will excuse me, good brother Janssen, I will go home now."

"Why, why—" Father began to stammer. "Is there something else the matter? You can be frank with me."

Richard edged closer. What did this man know?

The plowman glanced behind him. "No, no. All is just as I say. Folks can't be too careful these days. Excuse me, kindly."

Richard watched others come up, each with a different excuse.

"What's the matter with everyone, Father?"

Father stared over the field. "I don't know, and yet there can be only one answer. Someone has found out we're hiding Anabaptists—and they're afraid of what the church will do." He pulled his large brown hat over his eyes and fingered the plow.

Otto sighed. "It's just like Münster. People stopped talking to us—people we thought were friends. Everybody is afraid of the Anabaptists, not just the Catholics but the evangelicals, too."

"I think it's very brave of Uncle Sigmund and Aunt Frieda to believe as they do," Richard said.

Father looked surprised, but pleased. "Would

you like to become one of the Brethren?''

Richard was honest. "I'd have to be braver than I am now."

"How about you, Otto?"

"I'm not quite sure." Otto kicked at a clod. "I don't think I want to be hunted all the time, but I admit you have to be pretty brave to join them."

Father patted the lean oxen. "Well, boys, if no one is going to help us, we'll have to plow the field by ourselves. I'm glad now that the Prince-Bishop didn't sell me another strip."

Richard noticed two men talking some distance away. "Look! Someone's coming to help you, Father," Richard said.

Father looked up. "Why, it's the Prince-Bishop's overseer. And there comes Mr. Schwartz, too."

"Oh, Father, what are they going to do?"

With an impatient gesture toward Mr. Schwartz, the overseer started toward Father. Mr. Schwartz followed. They stumbled along the fresh furrows. At each step they had to stop and knock off moist clods from their feet.

"Mr. Janssen?" the overseer questioned, out of breath.

Before Father could reply, Hugo Schwartz thrust himself forward. "What do you want with Mr. Janssen?" he asked. "He is wanted for questioning."

"And who are you?" the overseer asked.

"Hugo Schwartz."

"Ah-h-h-h-h." The overseer turned his full gaze on Mr. Schwartz. "I have been looking for you."

"For me? Why?" Mr. Schwartz wavered.

"Do you know who I am?"

"No."

"I'm the Prince-Bishop's overseer."

Mr. Schwartz faltered, "Be pleased to tell his reverence that we are working for the best interest of the church."

The overseer put two fingers to his mouth and whistled. From a clump of trees near the edge of the field four soldiers in red jerkins, peaked helmets, and long pikes came running. They, too, stepped over furrows and had to stop to shake off globs of earth. They were panting by the time they arrived.

"I just want to say," the overseer told Mr. Schwartz in icy tones, "that the Prince-Bishop has dispensed with unauthorized groups who purport to rid the parish of unwelcome tenants."

Hugo Schwartz swallowed several times. His face worked. "But we are doing this for the church."

"As far as you are concerned, the Prince-Bishop himself is the church. If you persist in your activities, he will have you banished."

To be championed openly was so unexpected that Richard grinned. Hugo Schwartz scowled, clenched his fists, and stalked off.

"You are Mr. Janssen?" The overseer continued as if there had been no interruption.

"Yes."

"The Prince-Bishop tells me you want to buy some of his land."

Father hesitated. Richard could see the question in his mind. Buy land now?

"Yes," Father said. "I petitioned him many

months ago."

"The Prince-Bishop is granting you this privilege, and in accordance with the usual custom, you can buy as much as you can plow tomorrow."

The overseer left.

Richard exclaimed in dismay. "But you'll have only two oxen."

Father was able to plow only a pitifully thin strip the next day. When the overseer returned, he had a grim, unfriendly expression. What had happened in the meantime? Richard asked himself. Was he angry because Father had not been able to plow, or was there some other reason? A new fear gnawed at Richard.

The overseer went with Father to the house,

waited for the money to be counted into his hand, and after recounting it twice, tucked it in a bag tied to his waist. Then he took out a scroll. "The Prince-Bishop is concerned about those who have consorted with, aided, and comforted the secret sect of Anabaptists."

"But they are hard workers. They do not fight among themselves, and they pay their rents faithfully," Father said.

"That is true, but as Bishop of this parish, our Prince guides the spiritual lives of his flock. If one of the parish members sheltered an unbaptized baby, for example, it might go hard with him."

The overseer handed Father the scroll and left with a last warning. "The Prince-Bishop is determined not to tolerate Anabaptists or those in league with their pernicious beliefs."

Father did not reply.

After the overseer left, he broke open the embossed seal.

"What does the scroll say, Father?"

Father unrolled it and started to read. He flinched. His face turned ashy white. He put the scroll down on the table and rested his head in his hands.

Mother hurried to Father's side. "What's the matter, Thor? Are you ill?"

"It is nothing," Father put the scroll aside and would talk no more about it.

Richard turned away. Another secret. There were too many already.

6

TASTE OF EXILE

FOR several weeks Richard worried about the scroll, but did not mention it. Mrs. Walther visited once or twice. She seemed subdued, and even on one visit when she surprised Uncle Sigmund at his wood carving, she seemed to accept Mother's explanation of relatives visiting.

When Mr. Reinecke, the tall, stooped assistant pastor, announced that he would continue school for boys of the parish, Otto persuaded his parents to let him attend, along with Richard.

"I hope Mr. Reinecke is as good as the pastor who taught here before. He wasn't a bit stern," Richard said when they started down the road toward the Church of St. Mauritz.

Otto grinned. "You mean he didn't beat you every day?"

"He didn't beat anybody, but that wasn't the reason I liked him. He made everything sound interesting—even Latin."

Otto groaned in mock horror. "That's more than my teacher in Münster did. He used to make us drill out loud for hours. Sometimes I got so hoarse I couldn't talk above a croak."

A few minutes later, Richard pointed toward the apartments built off one side of the rounded bulk of the Church of St. Mauritz. "There's where we go."

He knocked at a door near the arched gateway. A tiny, shriveled woman hurried out, wiping her hands on her white apron. She motioned the boys toward the end of the hall.

In the bare schoolroom, ten or twelve boys sat on the straw-covered floor. Richard and Otto slipped down beside the others. When the schoolroom door opened a little later, all the boys sprang to their feet. Mr. Reinecke, tall and hollow-cheeked, climbed the tiny steps to the lectern in the corner, cleared his throat, and intoned several words in Latin. "Repeat after me," he ordered. The boys chanted in chorus.

The housekeeper came to the door and beckoned to Mr. Reinecke. He swallowed several times and left the room. When he returned, his face was pasty white. He adjusted his scholar's gown, anchored his flat cap on his head, and fumbled with the books.

What had upset Mr. Reinecke? The teacher sounded out the Latin lesson once more. The boys responded.

Someone flung the door open. Mr. Schwartz, his face red and swollen with rage, shook his fist at Mr. Reinecke. "Come out here at once."

The teacher's voice trembled. "Class dismissed. Go straight home. Do not discuss anything you see or hear—under penalty of twenty-five lashes." He tottered out.

Richard's head swam. What was there to discuss? One of the other boys turned and made the sign of the cross backward. Richard began to understand. Only the more daring boys made this gesture when they dared to imitate the fear-inspiring ceremony that cast a person out of the church—excommunication.

"If Mr. Reinecke's going to be excommunicated," a boy murmured, "I hope I get to see it."

Richard and Otto left the room with the others.

From a side room Mr. Schwartz' raspy voice rose in wrath. Mr. Reinecke answered in a shrill, high voice. A door slammed shut and muffled the voices.

There was no more school. Richard did not dare inquire about what had happened. He and Otto spent their days taking the parish cattle to the common pasture. Weeks passed. One morning Trudi met them on their way. "Go to church with me." She fingered her short cape with restless hands.

"Today? It isn't even open."

"Yes, it is. There's a special service. Mr. Reinecke's going to be excommunicated, and some other man. My father told me I had to go." She shivered. "He said it would be a lesson for me, but I want to see what an excommunication is like."

Richard felt a stir of excitement and a flush of shame. Here was a chance to see a man excommunicated from the church. But why had it happened to poor, trembling Mr. Reinecke?

"You go, Richard," Otto said. "We'd better not be seen together. I'll stay with the cattle."

Trudi agreed. "Yes, it would be safer. There's been a lot of talk lately against the Anabaptists. She flung back her head and stared over the fields. "Oh, why can't people be allowed to believe what they want to? It just makes me sick to hear Father talk the way he does. It makes me want to help all the Anabaptists in the world."

"Trudi, you think of the strangest things. Let's go."

They found the churchyard thronged. Richard could not remember seeing so many people all at once in his whole life. People who had not been to church for many months because of illness, now trembled over their canes, or leaned on others with eager, expectant expressions. Young mothers shifted their babies and hushed their cries. Men talked and nodded, or shook their heads.

"But where are there better citizens?" the parish miller demanded. "They bring thousands to the treasury and never take out a penny as officials. They set fire to no property. They do not use arms but nurse the wounded in the Prince-Bishop's wars."

"They are heretics," someone hissed. "They must be punished."

Two men unbolted the church doors. The people poured in. The Church of St. Mauritz filled to overflowing. Whole families, from grandfather to the smallest toddler, crowded into the pews. Young and old, sick and lame, gazed bright-eyed at the entrance near the pulpit.

61

Richard saw Mother near the front, gazing straight ahead. He and Trudi found a place to sit midway in the church.

Richard heard whispers around him.

"They say he recanted with his whole heart."

"Aye, and who wouldn't with the help of the whip?"

"Ssssh. Not so loud. It's true the whip is a great persuader."

The congregation rustled. Children, awed and silent, strained at the edge of the wooden benches and pointed to the shadowed entry.

A rustle at the doorway near the altar stilled every movement in church. A priest entered chanting in low tones. His full-skirted robes flowed with the rhythm of his step. Next a bishop entered. Assistants with lighted tapers followed and responded to the priest's chant with murmured responses.

The priest's oily phrases slid through the church. When the bishop mounted the pulpit, the priest raised his voice and ended on a triumphant note. He half-turned and waited.

Richard's head throbbed with the dread of something horrible and unknown. He heard a shuffling sound and a scraping of chains on the flagstone floor. Mr. Reinecke stood at the entrance, head bowed. He held a scroll in his right hand. His long tunic hung like lank flax about his sloping shoulders. Red spots pulsated on his cheeks, and when he looked up, his hooded eyes gleamed and burned from under craggy eyebrows. The priest signaled, and Mr. Reinecke sagged. Two guards pulled him into the church and placed him in an enclosure at the foot of the pulpit.

At a signal from the priest, Mr. Reinecke unrolled his scroll and began to read, "Of my own free will and in obedience to God's commandments, I hereby revoke and recant my heretical views about baptism."

His voice broke several times. The syllables quivered as if he had spoken the words under water. He paused, swayed to and fro like a reed before the wind. When the guards dragged him out, Mr. Reinecke's heels thumped on the flagstone floor.

A sigh rose from all over the church, a sigh of disappointment, as though people had been cheated out of a spectacle. Richard felt a spasm of disgust and a twinge of pity for the assistant for not having the courage to hold to the Anabaptist belief. Yet if he, Richard, were up there, would he have the courage to testify for Christ like the Anabaptists? Before he could answer his own question, he saw another man in the doorway. Father! Now he knew what the mysterious scroll meant—the summons for excommunication. But would Father recant like the assistant? No, he must not. He must hold firm in the new faith. Richard half rose, feeling somehow that if he could stand by Father's side, he could help, but immediately the people behind shoved him down. There was total silence in the church. Not one baby cried.

For the first time in his life, Richard prayed a personal prayer to God. "God, grant my father the courage to hold to what he believes."

Father unrolled his scroll.

"God, do not let this happen to my father," Richard prayed between clenched teeth. "You can help him. He is only trying to do Your will."

His arm ached. Only then he realized Trudi had been gripping it with all her strength.

Richard shut his eyes in a desperate last

appeal to God to give Father strength. His whole
body felt like a living arrow shot straight through
to God Himself.

Father started to read from the scroll. Then
the unseen hand of God seized him. With head
flung back, Father shouted, "I do not recant.
Infant baptism is not of God. Men must be
baptized by faith in Christ."

The congregation gasped and surged forward. The priest hissed commands. Two guards
sprang into the enclosure and wrenched Father
backward. His shout rang out, "If I weaken from
human weakness, by sword, fire, or water, may

God let me not depart from this life without faith. This I pray...."

A guard flung his arm around Father's throat and cut off the words.

The priest and the bishop talked in low tones.

Then the bishop seized a cross and swung it above his head like an unsheathed sword.

"By the authority of God the Father Almighty, we excommunicate and deliver over to the devil this malefactor, Thor Janssen. Accursed be he in towns, in fields, in highways, in footpaths, under roof, out of doors, and in all other places, standing, sitting, lying down, rising up, walking, running, awake, asleep, eating, drinking, and doing whatsoever other thing. From the illumination and all other things of the church we debar him; to the devil we condemn him, and in the pains of hellfire, we extinguish his soul."

Chilled and shaken, Richard fought down a smothering fear.

The bishop flung down the cross and seized a candle from the altar and shouted, "Just as this candle is deprived of its light, so let Thor Janssen be deprived of his soul in hell." He dashed the candle to the flagstone floor. The assistants flung theirs down. At once the church bells tolled.

"You may not enter the church again," the bishop went on in relentless tones. "No other Christian may associate with you." He raised his arms. "Let no man speak to him. As this light has been extinguished in the presence of all the community, so may the light of this life be extinguished before the face of Him who liveth forever."

The guards pushed Father out. The people pressed near the walls. Women held their skirts back, as if a touch might poison them.

Richard leaped up and followed his father through the narrow lane between the people. Someone stepped to his side. It was Mother. Hatred and fear rose like a hot wind on both sides. Outside Father stopped in the churchyard. While Richard and Mother caught up with him, people poured out of the church and scattered on each side. Trudi stood near, a sorrowing look on her pretty face. Someone hissed at Father. One woman spat.

Most of the congregation left, but some remained, as if wanting to help but afraid to. There was nothing to do now but go home. The Janssens walked in silence down the road.

At the farmhouse, several soldiers stood in the yard, holding pikes.

Father quickened his steps. "What are you doing here on my property?"

"We have been ordered to let no one in," a soldier said in clipped tones.

"But this is my home. I'm Thor Janssen. I've lived here for years—"

"Sorry. It isn't your home anymore. It has been confiscated."

"By whom?"

"The Prince-Bishop."

A knot of grief, anger, and rebellion tightened Richard's chest.

Mother clasped her hands and stared at the soldiers. "But where are we to go?"

"That is not our concern."

"May we get our clothes?"

"You may not go in."

"But this is madness—it isn't right." Father took a step toward the house.

At once the helmeted men leveled their long pikes.

"We have orders to kill anyone who tries to enter. Now be off with you," the leader said.

Mother stood with bowed head. Richard sprang to her side. A bitter truth rolled in his mouth. The Janssens had neither church nor home. Was this what God wanted when He tested men and asked them to give up everything for His sake?

Richard twisted away from the look of anguish on his parents' faces. Was he the one responsible? Hadn't he let Otto in, knowing that he was an Anabaptist? It was too late now. His decision weeks ago had made the whole family outcasts.

7

STRANGER WITH A MESSAGE

THE Prince-Bishop's soldiers paced in front of the Janssen farmhouse. There was no sound from within. Had Uncle Sigmund, Aunt Frieda, and the boys been turned out? Where would they all go now that both families had nothing but the clothes on their backs?

Father echoed Richard's thoughts. "Neither home nor church. Gone. Now we are entirely in God's hands."

To Richard's surprise, Father added, "But I feel a strange peace. For the first time in my life, I feel I am following God's commandment." Mother agreed.

"But what are we going to do now?" Richard asked in bewilderment. Yet he had to admit he felt a strange excitement, determination, a newborn trust in God. Would He not surely show the way?

A loud shout startled the family. Mr. Schwartz, his face red and puffy, ran up and shook his fist in Father's face. "You—you and that son of yours are to blame." Mr. Schwartz almost choked with rage.

"For what?" Father asked with weary calm.

"The Prince-Bishop's men seized my house and my land. They think I'm one of the accursed Anabaptists. I hate you Anabaptists with all my heart, and God will justify me."

"I'm sure He will," Father said in a mild tone.

Mr. Schwartz glared. "It was your conniving with the Anabaptists that started it all—harboring runaways. Oh, yes, I know all about it. Mrs. Walther told me everything. And now the Prince-Bishop thinks I'm a traitor even after I told his overseer all about you." Mr. Schwartz paused for breath.

Then that was why Father received the scroll for excommunication, Richard thought.

"You'll pay dearly for my losses. I'll see to that."

As he spoke, two horsemen galloped up. Richard recognized the Prince-Bishop's overseer. The other man was fully armed with long spurs, arm guards, embroidered gauntlets, and a vizor with plumes of purple and white feathers. An elaborately carved leather headpiece covered his horse's head and muzzle.

"It's the Prince-Bishop," Mr. Schwartz gasped.

"Who is this man?" the Prince-Bishop asked his overseer.

"Your Highness, this is the man Schwartz I told you about. You now own his house and land."

"Oh, yes. Serves him right."

Mr. Schwartz shrank back. "But Your Worship, I have done nothing. I am innocent."

"He says he is innocent," the overseer said.

"Innocent of what?" the Prince-Bishop asked with amused indifference.

Mr. Schwartz spoke directly to the Prince-Bishop. "I'm not an Anabaptist."

The overseer flicked him with a whip. "Speak to me. I'll convey the message," he said.

"I'm not an Anabaptist. I am a loyal, humble subject—"

The Prince-Bishop raised a gauntleted hand. "Tell him that you'll listen to his complaints." He glanced toward the Janssens. "Why are those people standing in the road?"

"That's Mr. Janssen and his family." The overseer spoke as if the family were not there. "He was excommunicated this morning for harboring Anabaptists."

"But he isn't one himself?"

"No, Your Highness."

They didn't know about Father's baptism. Hope sprang up in Richard. Maybe if Father kept silent, the Prince-Bishop would give back the Janssens' house. But Father was already speaking.

"Tell the Prince-Bishop that I am an Anabaptist."

After a shocked silence, the Prince-Bishop leaned forward and spoke directly to Father.

"Do you realize what you are saying?"

"Yes," Father answered. "I have lost all my material possessions because of my beliefs. Do you wish my life, too?"

The Prince-Bishop did not answer. He turned to the overseer. "Didn't this man buy some land from me?"

"Yes, Your Highness."

"I remember. You gave him a summons for excommunication instead of a deed of sale?"

"That is correct," the overseer said.

"I had wondered about my decision. I see that it was correct. These people must learn not to defy the church. Sell the land to someone else—to this man Schwartz, if you find him innocent."

Mr. Schwartz' face blazed in triumph, then fell. "I am innocent, but I have no money like some people."

The Prince-Bishop shrugged and wheeled his horse. He and the overseer rode away. Mr. Schwartz left, too. The Janssens stood alone.

A little boy ran up to them. "The 'postle is coming! The 'postle is coming."

"The what?" Richard recognized the miller's son.

"The 'postle." The little boy stamped his foot in annoyance. "Don't you know what a 'postle is?"

"Oh, you mean apostle."

"That's what I said."

Richard glanced down at the child's sparkling blue eyes. "Where is he?" he asked, in a half-hearted attempt to play the game.

The boy waved his hand. "Down the road, and he's got a long robe and a long beard, clear down to here." He reached to his knees. "And he has a curved staff as high as high." He reached up on tiptoe, almost dancing with importance.

"How do you know he's an apostle?"

"My father told me so."

"Where is he going?"

The little boy looked uncertain and dug his foot into the ground. "I don't know," he admitted. Then he clapped his hand to his mouth. "I wasn't supposed to tell anything." He ran off, calling over his shoulder, "Don't you tell."

A few minutes later a tall, long-bearded man plodded up the road. He planted his staff at every step with a firmness that somehow seemed impressive. He nodded pleasantly, then looked again. "You are in deep trouble, are you not?"

Father's stunned expression was answer enough. "Why, yes, but how could you know?"

"I have been with many who are in trouble," the man said. "Perhaps through God's power I can be of help to you. What has happened?"

"I have been excommunicated and the Prince-Bishop has confiscated my house and lands."

"What had you done against the church?" the traveler leaned on his staff and peered at Father with intense interest.

"I do not believe in child baptism," Father said.

The traveler smiled and nodded. "I thought it must be something like that. May I ask how you came by this belief?"

Richard drew in a quick breath. Now at last he would hear Father's story.

"From my brother. I didn't believe him at first, but when we studied the Bible I found that it nowhere mentions child baptism, and I realized that the so-called church is not the true church. Still, I do not believe in violence, and I would have gone on quietly learning more in my own way, but someone reported to the church authorities. My brother belongs to the so-called Ana-

baptists, and his family were staying with us, and
—" Father pointed to the soldiers guarding the
house. "You can see for yourself. No church, no
house, no lands. This is God's will."

"I have been with a man in Friesland who
has thought long about these things." The traveler
thumped his staff for emphasis. "He was a priest,
but he left the church. He has received much light
concerning the true baptism."

Friesland? Where had Richard heard that word
before?

"What is this man's name?" Father asked.

"Menno Simons."

Then Richard remembered. "Oh, Father, that's
the man the new pastor was talking about—"

The traveler interrupted. "Ah, that's the very
man I'm seeking." His eyes gleamed with satisfaction. "Where can I find him?"

"Nobody knows now. The soldiers took him
away."

The traveler's eyes dulled. He looked down.
"I see. All over Germany the faithful have sacrificed their lives for their beliefs. But I must not
go back to Menno Simons with empty hands.
Do you know of others like you?"

Richard remembered the baptism scene in the
Prince-Bishop's woods—the clearing, the stream,
the secret church. Of course. The meeting place
of Anabaptists who worshiped or who needed a
place to hide.

Richard tugged at Father's jerkin. "Tell him
about the church in the woods."

"How do you know about that?" Father
exclaimed.

"I—we saw you baptized. We didn't mean to.

We were going to make a hiding place—" Richard glanced toward the woods. "That's where Otto and the others must have gone! Let's go and see."

Richard was right. Not only Otto and his family were there, but also a few others, including the miller, who had brought grain to be stored as food for Anabaptists fleeing persecution.

Everyone greeted Menno Simons' messenger with hungry questions. "If we go to him, will he teach us?" they asked.

"He will turn none away," Menno's messenger assured them. "But remember, he is being hunted himself, and his whereabouts must be kept secret. But if you seek in God's name, you will find him."

While the others talked, Richard drew Otto to a fallen log. "How did you get away?"

Otto laughed and teased, "You'd never guess."

"Otto, tell me. We saw the soldiers there with those long pikes." Richard shuddered at the memory.

"Trudi came before they did and warned us."

"She did?" Richard marveled at Trudi's courage. "How did she know?"

"She heard her father talking to some men of the parish. But listen, Richard, can you think of a way we can get into the house again? My father says he left a list of names sewed in the lining of his jerkin. If the Prince-Bishop gets hold of those names, he'll confiscate the houses of all the people on the list. Think of a way to get back into the house."

Near them, Menno Simons' messenger gathered the little group together like a congregation. "Our belief has not been crushed by any means," he told them. "Anabaptist is a name despised by people who know nothing of the true belief, but this has not stopped the belief of the brethren over Germany, The Netherlands, Switzerland. Many have suffered death at the hands of their persecutors, yet believers are swelling our ranks by the hundreds every day. If we hold together in this belief, even though we may be separated from each other in the body, nothing can separate us from God or withstand God's will."

"Amen," the people murmured.

"We must not invite persecution by strange and unnatural actions. We will not rant nor rave nor persuade by force. We must arm ourselves with peace, not weapons. We must not provoke others to attack, but at the same time, we will gird ourselves with endurance, courage, and above all, faith."

While Menno Simons' messenger talked, the list that Otto mentioned kept coming back to Richard's mind. A list like that would certainly provoke attack. How could he and Otto get those names? Why not wait until dusk and break in? Otto instantly agreed.

At dusk some of the group went back to their homes. Others brought food and bedding for the Janssens.

"We'd better not tell anyone we're going back to the house," Otto warned Richard later. "It would just upset everyone."

As they crept across the field, they saw that the soldiers had built a campfire, and even at a distance their voices carried to the boys.

"They're drunk," Otto exclaimed. "That will make it easier."

Sure enough, they found two guards in the backyard stretched out in a drunken stupor. The boys stepped over them and entered the house.

"Where did Uncle Sigmund leave his jerkin?" Richard whispered.

"Upstairs, I think," Otto whispered back.

Once upstairs, it did not take long to find the jerkin. Richard thrust it in Otto's hands. "We might as well take some clothes and bedding back—and some food."

Being in the house with roaring soldiers outside gave Richard a sense of daring he did not know he possessed. He packed and sorted clothes and bedding with feverish haste. He heard footsteps below. Otto must have gone downstairs.

"Who's that?" Otto's voice right behind him made Richard jump. "There's someone else in the house." The boys listened to the stealthy steps, first a few at a time, then a pause, then a few more. It did not sound like a drunken soldier.

"What's he doing?" Richard whispered.

"I don't know. We'll just have to wait."

"Stay here. I'm going downstairs." Richard groped his way down and waited behind the door. Faint rustlings made his ears tighten. Had someone seen them come in? Was the intruder getting ready to attack? Richard held his breath until his head pounded. He heard heavy breathing, and sensed the intruder's nearness.

"Now!" he heard a man rasp under his breath. It sounded like Mr. Schwartz, but that was impossible. Richard heard running steps toward the back of the house, then silence. He did not dare move yet. He began to feel uncomfortably warm. The drunken soldiers must have put more

fuel on their campfire. A faint, crisp crackling
puzzled him. With infinite care, he peeked out. A
bright, orange glare made him blink in surprise.
Had a drunken soldier opened the front door?
Then he realized what was happening.

"Otto!" he called. "The house is on fire."

Otto hurried down with his arms full of clothing. Flames shot up from a pile of shavings near the front door. From every corner of the room, piles of shavings blazed. The boys batted the flames in frenzy, but when they extinguished one blaze, another sprang up twice as high.

Whoever had laid the fire with such care wanted the whole house and everything in it destroyed.

8

PAINFUL DECISION

RICHARD grabbed the loose jerkin from Otto's hands and beat down the flames nearest the kitchen door. Otto kicked at the burning shavings and stamped them out. The boys worked in desperate silence.

Outside a girl's voice rose in frantic appeal. "Wake up! Get up!" Richard heard the girl plead. "My father's in there."

Richard straightened up and stared at Otto. "That sounds like Trudi. What's she doing here?"

"Wake up!" Trudi implored.

"Wh—what?" a guard answered in a drunken grumble. "Go away. Don't bother us. We're guarding this house for the Prince-Bishop. No one can go in."

"But don't you understand? The house is on fire and my father's inside. Help me get him out."

"Go away, Miss. Nobody's in that house. We've been here all day."

"I tell you my father's in there." Trudi's

hysterical insistence reached a frenzy. "I followed him here, and I saw him go in. If you don't help me, I'll go in myself."

She pushed the door part way open. A shower of sparks flew up. Trudi gasped and backed out. Richard saw her undo her neck scarf and put it around her face. Behind her, the guards stirred and grumbled. Richard did not want them to see him, and he did not want Trudi to come in.

"Keep her out," Otto said. "It's too dangerous."

The door bumped open. Trudi, her eyes big behind the scarf, stumbled in. Richard caught her arm. "Don't give us away, Trudi. Otto and I are the only ones here. We're trying to put the fire out." He forestalled her question. "Your father isn't here."

Trudi stood so still that Richard wondered if shock had numbed her senses.

"I'll help you," she said with determined abruptness.

Even with her help, the two boys could not control the flames. They brought down armloads of bedding and clothes before the fire shot up the narrow stairway.

"It's no use," Richard said. "We'll have to leave whether the guards see us or not."

"Don't worry about that part," Trudi answered. "The guards are dead-drunk." She coughed from smoke and rubbed her streaming eyes. "But where will you go? Where are the others?"

"In the woods."

"You mean where we found the secret church?"

Trudi's open astonishment nettled Richard. "Of course. Where else could we go and not be found out?"

Otto interrupted. "We can't waste any more time. Trudi, will you go outside and distract the guards if they're awake? We'll make a dash for the field with as much as we can carry in one load."

Trudi nodded and ran outside. Richard heard the guards mutter, but they seemed too drunk to know what was going on. Richard and Otto each grasped a bundle of clothing and dashed to a safe distance from the house. Trudi caught up with them. Otto fumbled through the pile of clothes. "Where's the list, Richard? It was in Father's jerkin."

With a rueful grin, Richard handed over the battered leather garment. "I used it to fight the fire. But the list is safe inside the lining. It didn't get burned."

They looked back at the burning house. The kitchen door burst outward and a sheet of flame lit up the yard. The guards woke with a yell and scrambled to their feet. In a few minutes all the Prince-Bishop's soldiers were running about shouting directions and bumping into each other.

"What will the Prince-Bishop do when he finds his new house burned?" Otto mused. "He'll blame the guards for it."

Richard nudged Otto in warning. Otto must not let Trudi find out that they knew her father had set the fire.

Trudi burst into tears. "Father burned the house, Richard. He filled a sack with shavings. I followed him over here. I saw him go in." She swallowed hard. "The guards were sitting around drinking." She watched the soldiers fight the fire for a few minutes in silence.

"And then what?" Richard asked.

"When Father didn't come home to supper, I came back. By that time the house was blazing." She wrung her hands. "Oh, why doesn't Father let the Anabaptists alone? But he hates them, and he says he'll track down their secret church."

"But didn't the Prince-Bishop take away your father's house because he thought your father was Anabaptist?"

"That's just it. Father will redouble all his efforts now to prove to the Prince-Bishop that he's loyal to the church." She added, "Loyal! Maybe he is, but I think he's doing terrible things. I just don't know what to think or do. If the Prince-Bishop finds out that Father set the fire, I don't know what will happen."

Otto took her arm. "The best thing for you to do now, Trudi, is go back to Mrs. Walther's and act as if nothing had happened."

Richard agreed. "No one has to know about your father. We won't tell, and don't you tell on us, Trudi. All of us would be in more trouble than we know how to handle." He heaped an armload of clothing on a blanket, tied the four corners together, and slung the bundle over his shoulder. "We're going back to the woods."

Trudi gasped. "You can't go now. Look over there! Everyone in the neighborhood is coming to see the fire."

They all turned toward the burning house. "Someone must have aroused the entire parish," Otto said. "How would they have known about it otherwise?"

People milled about at a safe distance to

watch the fire. The burning house gripped Richard with a morbid, tingling fascination. It hurt him to see the house burn, yet he could not turn away. "Otto, let's separate and mix with everyone. Don't let anyone see us together. Maybe we can find out what's going to happen next. Trudi, you keep your ears open, too." Richard pushed his bundle under a bush. "We'll get this later."

The three separated and went toward the blaze. Richard joined the spectators near the front of the house.

A little girl pulled at her mother's skirts. "Mother, are they going to burn everybody's house?"

"No, of course not. Just the bad, bad houses."

"What did the house do that was bad?"

"Nothing. The house didn't do anything."

"But Mother—"

"It wasn't the house. Bad people lived here —Anabaptists." The mother lowered her voice and whispered the last word.

"Then why are they hurting the house?" the child persisted.

The mother jerked her daughter away. "We must go home."

"But I want to see it burn," the child wailed.

Richard looked at former friends and neighbors clustered about the burning house. He saw excitement mingled with fear written on their faces. How could they help but think it was God's punishment? Mr. Schwartz strutted back and forth, his short, square figure silhouetted against the blaze. Was it for the sake of the church that he set fire to the house—or was it revenge against Father? In his heart, Richard knew the answer.

Three people, including Trudi, his own daughter, knew that Mr. Schwartz had set the fire. If the Prince-Bishop found out, Mr. Schwartz would be severely punished, perhaps imprisoned in a dungeon.

Richard listened to the comments of the spectators.

"Best-built house in all the parish."

"Yes, Mr. Janssen is a fine carpenter."

"Too bad he turned Anabaptist," someone said. "Excommunicated, lands taken away, house destroyed—"

"Maybe he set it on fire himself," a neighbor suggested.

"No, not Mr. Janssen," people exclaimed on all sides.

"Heretic or not, with his strange views on baptism, he's honest," someone said.

Another said in a low voice, "That Mr. Schwartz, with all his parading—I don't trust him."

Richard felt a nudge at his elbow. Otto thrust a jerkin into Richard's hands. "Take this to the woods as fast as you can. It's the list."

The note of urgency was not lost on Richard. "Why the hurry? What happened?"

"Mr. Schwartz overheard me talking to Trudi about the names, and he wants the list. I've dodged him for a minute. He thinks I'm you. Don't let him see us together."

Richard did not stop to question. He took the jerkin and started toward the woods. But a new commotion stopped him. The Prince-Bishop's overseer, flanked by a dozen soldiers on horseback, rode up. People scattered to a safe distance and stood in a ragged half circle, their faces strained and fearful.

"You drunken soldiers!" The overseer snapped his whip. "Why did you set Mr. Schwartz' house on fire?"

Mr. Schwartz ran up and caught the bridle of the overseer's horse. "I am Mr. Schwartz," he said. "This isn't my house. It belongs to Thor Janssen, the heretic."

"It was to have been your house tomorrow, by the Prince-Bishop's orders. He has found out your loyalty to the church and took this way to reward you." The overseer shook his head. "Too bad. This was the finest house in the parish. But don't worry. It will go hard with these drunken soldiers for setting it on fire."

Mr. Schwartz' face sagged in ashy dismay. "My house! My own house!" he half-whispered.

A soldier flung himself on his knees before the overseer. "We didn't burn the house." He turned to his companion. "Did we?"

"No, sir, we did not burn it. But we know the person who did."

"Who, then? Be quick with your answer."

The soldier pointed to Trudi. "There's the one who did it. I saw her go into the house."

"Trudi!" A strange mixture of anxiety and horror mottled Mr. Schwartz' face. "Mr. Overseer, this is my daughter. She couldn't possibly have set the fire." He gripped Trudi's shoulder and shook her until she cried out in pain. "Say you weren't even here."

Trudi wrenched herself free. "I did not set the fire." Her biting scorn curbed Mr. Schwartz' outburst. "But I was here."

Mr. Schwartz stepped back. His mouth worked, but no sound came out.

"There, you see?" The guard wiped his forehead with the back of his hand.

"It isn't true. My daughter could not have set the fire." Mr. Schwartz looked around with a frantic, glazed expression. "She wouldn't know how." He checked himself and pointed to Otto. "There's the boy who did it—Richard Janssen, the son of the Anabaptist heretic. His father set him to it. That's the boy you want."

"Bring the boy to me," the overseer said.

Two men dismounted, seized Otto, and brought him before the overseer.

Richard watched from the shadows, dazed. His thoughts whirled. Should he speak up and say he was Richard? But he had the list of names tucked in his tunic. What if the overseer ordered him searched? The Prince-Bishop would get hold of the list and many lives would be endangered. It would be better to take the list to Uncle Sigmund.

But what would happen to Otto? Could he leave him to face questioning, perhaps punishment and imprisonment?

What was the right decision this time? Which action would do the most good? With painful clarity, Richard knew he was thinking of others, but that didn't make the decision come any easier.

What did God want him to do?

9
THE BRIBE

I'LL take the list back, Richard decided, yet he lingered to watch the Prince-Bishop's soldiers fight the fire. The chimney fell with a thunderous crash. Sparks rained on the spectators. As they scrambled out of the way, Richard saw Otto break away and dive headlong into the darkness. The Prince-Bishop's men shouted, and their horses reared and whinnied. Two horsemen ran to mount their horses.

"Let him go," the overseer shouted. "Stay here and put out this fire."

Spurred by both hope and fear, Richard ran after Otto and caught up with him at the edge of the woods. Both boys flung themselves on the ground panting.

"What'll we do now?" Richard asked. "We'll never find our way through the woods in the dark."

"We'd better stay right here the rest of the night," Otto decided.

At daybreak the two boys made their way

to the clearing and poured out the story of the fire.

Mother did not weep. "It is all in God's hands," she kept saying, and her calm face showed her complete faith.

Uppermost in everyone's mind was where they could live.

"I would like to go to Friesland," Father said. "This Menno Simons we have heard about sounds like a true leader."

"What about Strasbourg?" Uncle Sigmund suggested. "Melchior Hofmann has over two thousand followers even though he has been in prison for ten years."

He and Father pored over the list of names the boys had brought back.

"Is it a map, too?" Richard asked.

"No, just names of Brethren and the districts they live in. One family will pass us on to another family a day's walk ahead," Uncle Sigmund explained. "But it will be safer if we travel in two groups half a day apart."

The two families decided to go to Friesland and ask Menno Simons to be their pastor. After earnest prayers for guidance and safekeeping, Uncle Sigmund and his family left first. But at noon Otto came back.

"The road to Friesland is blocked. The Prince-Bishop's soldiers have camped right on it. We'll have to go to Strasbourg, now." Otto sat on a log and tried to catch his breath. "Follow us about midafternoon," he said when he left.

When it was time to go, Richard acted as scout to see if the road was clear. To his horror, he saw swarms of the Prince-Bishop's horsemen blockading the road to Strasbourg. He ran back to tell Father and Mother.

"But what are we to do?" Mother asked in bewilderment. "We can't live here in the woods. Where can we go?"

"There's one place no one thought of," Richard said.

"Where?"

"Münster."

"Münster?" Mother echoed. "We can't go there. We wouldn't be safe at all."

But Father agreed with Richard. First, the church authorities would not expect such boldness. Second, in such a big town the family could surely live without calling attention to themselves. They could keep their religious beliefs a secret.

Going to Münster proved easier than Richard expected. Father remembered names of Brethren from Uncle Sigmund's list, and with their help he established a carpenter shop on a side street not far from the cathedral and its adjoining market place. The Janssens settled into rooms over the shop.

"You'll have plenty of work," one of the Brethren, a blacksmith on the same street, told Father.

He spoke the truth. In a short time orders for shelves, cupboards, stools, chests, window frames, and doorposts poured in. Soon the carpenter shop became the planning center for secret meetings of the Brethren. Each worship service had to be held at night in a different place each time—a garret, the back of a shop, or even by the stream in the center of town.

89

One afternoon Richard hurried over the cobbled, winding streets to leave word with various Brethren that a worship meeting would be held that night at the blacksmith's shop. He ducked his head against the biting wind and almost ran into a girl huddled against one of the columns of an arcade. The girl raised frightened eyes, then gasped, "Why, Richard Janssen, what are you doing here?"

Richard stared. Could this be Trudi? This girl with the white face and thin, pinched cheeks? "Trudi, never mind about me, I'll explain later. Why are *you* in Münster?"

A shadow crossed her face. "I've run away from Father, Richard. I'm never going back."

"But what will you do? How will you live?"

"I'll find work here with some family." She paused. "Richard, are you one of the Brethren now?"

The abruptness of her question startled him. "Father and Mother are," he hedged.

"I mean you, Richard. Have you been re-baptized?"

Somehow Trudi always managed to touch on a sore point, Richard reflected. Why hadn't he been baptized? He couldn't explain why, but he told Trudi how he acted as messenger for the Brethren's secret church. He hoped she wouldn't probe further.

90

Trudi rushed on. "I want to be one of the Brethren. It's what God wants me to do. I've felt this for a long time, but I just couldn't find the courage to leave Father." She shivered and put her hand on Richard's arm. "Richard, won't you be baptized with me?"

Richard swallowed in embarrassment. For weeks the Brethren had gathered for secret worship, first at one house, then another. Mother had been baptized. Richard believed in their principles. Why couldn't he say yes to Trudi?

Trudi's hand felt icy cold on his arm. "Trudi, you're ill," he said. "You can't stay here. Come home with me."

Trudi did not protest.

Mother put Trudi to bed at once and nursed her until she recovered. "There's no reason why she should work for some strange family," Mother told Richard later.

"Oh, Mother, I was hoping you would say that. Then she can live with us?"

"Of course. Poor, motherless girl."

In a short time it seemed as if Trudi had always been part of the family. She studied the Word of God with the family and went to the secret meetings of the Anabaptists.

"I'll be baptized when you are, Richard," she told him one night when the family had returned from a worship service. "When are you going to take your stand for God?"

"Don't push me, Trudi," Richard said. "It's as if I had to wait for something. I don't know how to explain it."

Trudi nodded. "I know what you mean. I won't say any more, but you let me know when you're ready and we can be baptized together."

Will I really know when the time comes? Richard asked himself. *How will I be able to tell?*

One day the blacksmith came upstairs with ominous news. "There's a new committee being

formed. They're going to track down all the Anabaptist brethren who are left here in Munster. It's exile or worse for those who are caught."

"Do you think we should try to meet in secret anymore?" Mother asked.

"Let's let the others have a chance to express their views," Father said. "We'll have the meeting here tonight."

Father sent Richard with the message for the Anabaptists. "They must all come. It may mean life or death."

Richard started on the familiar rounds. Near the Church of St. Lamberti he passed a stocky man with a familiar strut. Richard glanced back in panic. What was Mr. Schwartz doing in Münster? Had he tracked down Trudi? Or was he working on the committee with his deadly hatred of the Anabaptists? More important, had Mr. Schwartz recognized him? The question nagged Richard.

On impulse, Richard slipped around the Church of St. Lamberti and watched Mr. Schwartz go to the Town Hall a little way up the street. What was he going to the Town Council for? Richard kept out of sight and waited until Mr. Schwartz came out. Several burghers came out, too, and talked to Mr. Schwartz. Several of the Prince-Bishop's soldiers lounging nearby straightened up and approached the group.

Richard was puzzled. Could this be the new committee? He hurried home, wondering whether to tell Trudi or just hope that Mr. Schwartz hadn't recognized him—or, worse yet, followed him. At home he didn't have to make a decision. Both Mother and Trudi were out, probably at the market stalls nearby, he thought.

Someone knocked. Who could it be? Richard braced himself behind the door and cautiously slid back the bolt. In the dim light, Richard saw the outline of a boy his own size. He shouted in recognition. "Otto! Where did you come from?"

Otto hurried in, his face grim. "Yes, it's Otto. Something terrible has happened. Mr. Schwartz has the list of names."

"How *could* he? Start at the beginning, Otto."

The leader in Strasbourg had died a few weeks before, Otto explained.

"Then we found out that you were here, and we decided to come back."

"But how did you know we were here?" Richard interrupted.

"Traveling Brethren passed the word along," Otto said and continued his story. In Münster they looked up people on the list. His parents were at the blacksmith's. "I came on ahead to find your place. It was unbelievable, but Mr. Schwartz appeared from nowhere and grabbed the list. Before I knew it he was gone. How could such a thing happen? I just can't understand it."

Richard broke in. "I can." He told of meeting Mr. Schwartz, of following him to the Town House. "And the Prince-Bishop's soldiers will probably make a house-to-house search," he added. Then a wholly new idea struck him like a blow. "He must have turned the list over to the Town Council."

Otto groaned. The boys did not talk much until Mother and Trudi returned and heard the story. Mother was quiet, and after her first gasp,

Trudi was silent, too.

"But I came to find out—do you have any room for us?" Otto asked.

"Of course. Go get your parents. Trudi and I will fix a place for all of you to sleep."

When the excitement of Uncle Sigmund's and Aunt Frieda's arrival had subsided, the two families discussed Mr. Schwartz' action.

"If the list is in the hands of the Town Council we won't have much time to plan," Father said, "but there's nothing we can do now."

While the grown-ups discussed plans for the meeting, Richard, Trudi, and Otto withdrew to the storeroom to talk. At the sound of footsteps on the stairs, Richard exclaimed, "That'll be the first of the Brethren."

Then he heard a gutteral, mocking greeting. Trudi clenched her fists and sprang to her feet. "It's Father! What am I going to do? Where can I hide?" She looked wildly around the room.

Otto pulled her down.

"Wait, Trudi. Let's listen first."

Richard heard Mr. Schwartz clear his throat, "There's no use hiding anything from me, Mr. Janssen," he said. "I followed your boy from house to house today."

Richard whispered, "Did he follow you or me?"

"It doesn't matter now," Otto whispered back. "But I think he'd be surprised to see us together."

"What do you want from us?" Richard heard Father ask. "Haven't you done enough to me and my family? We are law-abiding citizens here. We pay our debts and taxes."

"Mr. Janssen, you know that you Anabaptists

will be banished—or worse—if the Town Council finds out about you?"

"Yes, of course," Father said.

"Perhaps we can come to a little understanding. I have here a list of quite a number of your Anabaptist brethren—"

Richard heard the sound of a chair overturning. Father must have jumped up. "What are you saying?"

"Mr. Janssen, there is no reason why the Town Council must know everything. I will be glad to sell this list to you for a reasonable price. I can guarantee that you will not be molested. Otherwise—" he paused.

Otto and Richard stared at each other. Richard knew Otto was thinking the same thing he was. *Mr. Schwartz had already betrayed them to the council, but he hadn't told the council about the list of names.*

Before Richard or Otto could stop her, Trudi screamed, "No, no," and ran to the front room. Richard opened the door enough to peek through. Otto stood at his shoulder.

"I will not let you do this, Father." Trudi clenched and unclenched her fists.

Richard saw shocked surprise and unmistakable joy light Mr. Schwartz' face. 'Trudi! You're alive! I thought—" His face worked, then hardened. "So this is where you have been hiding. I should have guessed. Now, my girl, you keep out of men's business."

Trudi folded her arms. "Father, you are not going to take money, and you're going to hand over that list. If you do not, I will go to the Prince-Bishop and tell what you did." Her tone held an undercurrent of deadly meaning.

Mr. Schwartz blustered and fumed. "You don't know what you're talking about."

"Oh, yes, I do."

But Trudi must be thinking about her father burning the house. She didn't know he'd already betrayed the Janssens. Richard was in an agony of suspense. Should he speak or not?

Mr. Schwartz swallowed and looked from one person to another. A crafty expression crossed his face. "My girl, I'm your father. Don't forget that. You'll have to go home with me."

"It is true that you are my father, but I owe you nothing," Trudi said. "Especially now. Remember, the Prince-Bishop's dungeons are deep."

Mr. Schwartz sat down and buried his face in his hands. Was he thinking about his betrayal? If the soldiers came, they'd take Trudi, too.

"Come home with me," Mr. Schwartz pleaded. "You're all I have. Then I won't bother anybody. I promise."

For the space of a hundred heartbeats, Trudi stared at her father. "Very well. I'll go home with you. I'll get ready." She left the room.

Richard felt an emotional earthquake. Trudi, the level-headed one, so sure in her new faith! How could she give up all she believed in and go home with her father, a sworn enemy to the Anabaptists?

Yet Trudi had not hesitated to sacrifice herself to save the lives of her friends. *Would I do the same?* Richard asked himself. All the days and weeks of indecision flooded in his memory. Could he stand by and let Trudi make this sacrifice? He ran out to the front room.

"Mr. Schwartz," he began, "Trudi isn't going with you."

Mr. Schwartz scowled. "Why not?"

"Because—" Richard began. *Because you've already betrayed the family,* he was going to say.

"Richard, stop!" Trudi hurried in. "Do you want to spoil everything?" She held out her hand for the list.

With great reluctance, her father handed it to her.

Richard hesitated. The list was safe. Besides, how could he be sure that Mr. Schwartz had betrayed the Janssens?

He watched Mr. Schwartz and Trudi go downstairs. They passed a group of armed men on their way up.

"Where is Thor Janssen?" the first one called.

Father appeared at the door. "Here I am."

"By orders of the Prince-Bishop, we arrest you as one of the leaders of the heretical sect of Anabaptists." The first soldier turned to the ones behind him. "Take this man to the tower tonight and to the Town Hall tomorrow for interrogation."

The soldiers marched Father out. Trembling with shock, Richard leaned against the door frame. As the realization of his father's arrest sank in, he faced the tormenting thought: *If I had spoken, I could have saved Trudi. Because I didn't speak, I failed Trudi, Father, myself—and God.*

10

TRAP FOR HERETICS

RICHARD listened to sounds of shouts and scurrying feet. Close by, he heard Trudi's voice. The next moment she ran up the stairs, followed by her father.

Trudi whirled on him. "You'd already told the authorities before you came here. You knew the soldiers were on their way to arrest Mr. Janssen." Her eyes blazed. "And knowing that, you dared to ask for money and make me a promise you had no intention of keeping." Her lips curled. "I suppose you're going to tell me you did this for the church. Does God want you to lie, covet, and steal?"

Trudi's unexpected attack left Mr. Schwartz speechless.

"Father, I'm not going home with you," Trudi announced. "I am one of the Anabaptists now."

Her father took a step toward her. Trudi shrank back with a look of loathing.

"Don't you realize the Anabaptists are being

seized all over Germany?" A note of fear crept into Mr. Schwartz' pleading. "Many have been sentenced to death. Trudi, you're my daughter. You must come with me. I'll save you. No one need ever know that you had anything to do with these heretics." Mr. Schwartz pulled out a large, square handkerchief and mopped his forehead.

"I'll save the family, too," he babbled. "I'll talk to the council and explain. I'll—"

"Father, just go. Everything is in God's hands now."

With head bowed, Mr. Schwartz left. Trudi sat on the top step and cried into her apron. Richard did not know what to say.

Otto came out. "There's some kind of fighting going on near the market square. We've been watching out the window."

In a moment a man ran up the stairs. Richard recognized one of the Anabaptists.

"Where is Mrs. Janssen?" he panted.

When Mother came out, the Anabaptist leaned against the wall of the stairway and told his message between gasps for air. "Your husband is safe," he said. "We were coming to the meeting here, and we saw Mr. Janssen in the hands of soldiers. We all know that the persecution has started again, and we must not lie down like lambs to the slaughter."

"What happened? What did you do?" Mother pressed her hands together.

"We took him away from the soldiers by force, and some of the Brethren will hide him."

Mother's face glowed with hope. "What shall we do now? Do you think the soldiers will come back after us?"

The Anabaptist shook his head. "No one knows. We cannot keep Mr. Janssen hidden for more than a few hours. When he returns, I advise all of you to leave Münster."

When the Anabaptist left, the family gathered in the front room to discuss plans for leaving. Mother, Aunt Frieda, and Trudi sewed money into the lining of clothes and put enough cheese and grain in small pouches to last each person several days. Uncle Sigmund traced rough maps for each one.

"This time we must make our way to Friesland. Perhaps this is what God meant us to do all the time," he said. "Somehow I feel we will triumph over every obstacle."

With all the discussion for leaving, Richard knew everyone kept listening for Father's footsteps. When he did come a little after midnight, he did not explain where his friends had taken him. "There may be questions later. The less everyone knows, the better."

He approved of the plans to leave, and brought out a sack of coins Mother had not found. "I suspected something like this would happen sooner or later," he explained. "It will be much better if we can pay our way."

By dawn the family had finished preparations for the long trip to Friesland.

"We'll have to leave in full daylight," Father planned. "We'll gather up market baskets and appear to be farmers going home after a day of selling."

Otto brought up a question everyone had forgotten. "What about the list of names?"

101

Mother gave a shuddering sigh. "Can't you leave it with one of the Brethren here?"

"The blacksmith—he'll know what to do with it," Richard suggested.

Everyone agreed.

"I'll take it, and you follow me," Otto told Richard.

The two boys went downstairs, keeping a sharp lookout for the Prince-Bishop's soldiers. Otto started off and Richard followed. He saw Otto near the blacksmith shop and breathed a sigh of relief. The list would soon be out of their hands. Then to his shock, he saw Otto turn back, white terror on his face. Mr. Schwartz ran after him with relentless speed. Otto thrust the list in Richard's hands.

"He saw me take out the list—and he's after it. Take it and run in the other direction. He hasn't seen us. We can fool him yet."

Richard slipped the list in his tunic, but Mr. Schwartz was already on them. The two boys faced him. Mr. Schwartz looked from one boy to the other with incredulous dismay. "There are two of you."

Richard did not dare run now. To do so would let Mr. Schwartz know he had the list.

"Which one of you is Richard Janssen?"

The boys did not reply. Richard grinned. He sensed Mr. Schwartz' complete bafflement, and he knew that whichever direction he chose to run, Otto would choose the opposite. Which boy would Mr. Schwartz then choose to chase?

Richard caught Otto's glance and with a slight nod to each other, both boys started in opposite directions. Mr. Schwartz, with an

anguished glance over his shoulder at Richard,
started after Otto. Richard looked back in time
to see that Mr. Schwartz had changed his mind
and was running after Richard instead.

Now panic gripped him. The list felt bulky
under his tunic. Which way should he go? How
could he get rid of the names? He darted down the
winding streets he knew so well, dodged and ducked
into back alley ways and went in a circle back
to the blacksmith's. If he could just get rid of the
list, he didn't care what happened. He ran until
his legs felt like dry sticks.

But it was no use. A glance over his
shoulder showed Mr. Schwartz right behind
him. Richard cut across another street and
darted into the blacksmith's shop.

"Someone's after me," he called. The

blacksmith rose from a white-hot fire blazing in an open stone fireplace.

"I'll take care of him." The blacksmith ran to the doorway.

Where could he put the list? By the light of a white-hot fire, Richard searched the room for a hiding place. The wooden boxes with slanted sides wouldn't do. They were filled with horseshoes. Nearby a ladder reached up to a wide shelf, but it was too open a place to put the list. The only possibility was a big iron kettle on the floor near the fire. Richard slipped the list inside and replaced the lid. Heavy footsteps sounded outside. Richard ran behind the big wooden box.

He heard voices at the door. "But I saw him come into one of these doorways," he heard Mr. Schwartz roar. "Let me in." The words whistled on Richard's ears.

"You can't go in. It's too hot. I have a fire so hot I had to come outside for air myself. Let it cool down."

"I can't wait."

"You have no right to come into my shop. I forbid it."

Richard made a quick decision. Why not get rid of the list once and for all? He reached for the lid of the kettle. It slipped from his fingers and clanged to the floor. Both men whirled. Richard grabbed the list and bolted toward the fireplace. In one leap Schwartz caught him by his collar. "Hand over those names, Richard, or whoever you are. You boys have made a fool out of me for the last time."

Richard wrenched free and flung the scroll

into the white-hot fire. The names gleamed black for a second, crumpled, and disappeared forever.

The blacksmith picked up tongs that glowed white-hot at the tips. With a scowl and muttered threats, Mr. Schwartz backed out of the shop.

The Janssen families decided to leave by the familiar Mauritz gate. When the city walls loomed into view, Richard and Otto went ahead to scout. The city gate, usually open at this time of day, was closed.

The boys approached two guards.

"We would like to leave the city," Richard said.

One guard nudged the other. Big grins spread across both their faces.

"Of course, of course," one said with elaborate courtesy. "Any time. People are free to come and go. Angels guard the city."

The ironic tone bothered Richard.

"Aren't we free to leave? Is there any law against it?" Otto asked.

"No, no. No law at all. If you insist, you may leave. We'll open the inner gate and close it behind you, and then we'll open the outer gate. From then on, you'll be on your own."

His words sounded ominous.

"Is something happening out there?" Richard asked.

The guard nudged his partner again. "Is something happening? Tell you what. Shinny up that ladder there and see for yourself."

Richard and Otto climbed the ladder and stood on the parapet. On every side, hardly a stone's throw from the wall, swarms of men walked about, called to each other, or sat on stones and sharpened their weapons. Tents had sprung up, with red, yellow, and green pointed banners fluttering in the breeze. Fires dotted the fields. Here and there women stirred huge pots on tripods.

"Are they all the Prince-Bishop's soldiers?" Richard asked, although he knew the answer.

"Who else would they be?" the guard called.

A soldier looked up at the boys. "Jump down. We'll catch you." He held out his arms. His puffed sleeves and doublet of yellow, green, and black looked as wide again as the man. All the soldiers wore full, knee-length trousers, bright-colored jerkins, and metal helmets and carried long lances.

Richard gazed at the encampment, turned back.

"We can't leave."

"I wouldn't advise it," the guard said in a droll voice. "Did you see the angels?"

Richard turned away.

"They're in disguise, that's all," the guard called after him. "They look like the Prince-Bishop's paid soldiers, but they're really angels. They'll send all the heretics direct to heaven." The guards burst into laughter.

"What are they waiting for?" Richard asked.

"Why, my boy, they're waiting for Anabaptists. The Prince-Bishop tells us these heretics are on the rise again. He has soldiers stationed at each of the city gates. That way, he'll snag them all."

The boys climbed down.

"What's the matter? Don't you want to leave?" a guard asked.

"Not now," Richard faltered, and the guards guffawed.

The boys brought the disheartening news to the waiting families.

"But we don't dare go back," Mother exclaimed.

"And we can't go on, not with all the Prince-Bishop's soldiers out there," Richard said.

Where could they go now?

Richard watched the farmers, their wives, and children going home from the market. Whenever a large group gathered at the gate, the guards let them through. A tall wagon with sharply sloped sides creaked by.

"Couldn't we leave one by one?" he asked the others in excitement. "Otto and I could get a ride with some farmer, and—"

Father caught the idea at once. "That's just what we'll do. I believe we can all slip through safely if we don't stay together."

"Uncle Thor, couldn't we all meet at the secret church?" Otto asked. "We could wait for one another there."

"But what if something happens?" Aunt Frieda faltered.

"After two days, each one will have to make his way to Friesland as best he can." Father sounded decisive.

Both families agreed to the plan.

When another tall wagon slowed down near the gate, Richard and Otto asked the farmer for a ride. His suspicious glance alerted Richard. "Just as far as the Church of St. Mauritz."

The farmer thought for a moment and jerked his thumb over his shoulder. "I'll take one of you

107

but not both."

"You go first. I'll get on the next one."

Otto boosted Richard up. The wagon smelled of moldy hay and barnyard manure, but to Richard it smelled like freedom.

The wagon wheels screeched and jolted. Richard crouched on the rough floor boards. His heart pounded. Would he get through the city gates or not?

11

COURAGEOUS DECISION

THE wagon stopped with a lurch between the inner and outer gates.

"What's in your wagon?" he heard a guard ask.

"A runaway boy."

Richard choked back his terror. Why had the farmer betrayed him?

To his astonishment, the guard only laughed. "Pass on through."

Now Richard could hear loud talking and laughter and guessed the wagon was passing through the soldiers' camp. His fear subsided, and when the wagon halted, he leaped out. He was not far from the Church of St. Mauritz.

"Thank you, thank you," he called to the farmer.

"I said you were a runaway. I told the truth as I saw it. Now you tell the truth. Are you a runaway?"

"Yes, I am."

"Where are you heading?"

"To Friesland."

"What for?" The farmer sounded almost friendly.

"There's a man there that I'm supposed to find."

"Where are your parents?"

"They're waiting to leave Münster."

"What is this man's name?"

Should he answer? Somehow, Richard knew he should tell the truth.

"His name is Menno Simons."

"Ah-h-h." The long exhalation told Richard more than words.

"A messenger of his stayed at our house a while back. Since then I've had a lot of refugees cross my farm. It seems to be a handy place to hide, with so many trees and shrubs nearby. Come to the house. Let's see what the good wife might be having for us to eat."

The plump, bustling little farmer's wife did not appear surprised at her unexpected guest.

Soon Richard sat down to a supper of cheese made from ewe's milk, hot oat cakes, and baked apples. After the last mouthful Richard sighed in satisfaction.

The woman showed him a place to sleep. In the morning Richard tried to pay for his lodging, but the farmer waved it away.

"I never could believe these bits of metal stood for anything. You can't eat them or feed them to cattle."

"Then I'll help you with a day's work," Richard offered.

"No, I thank you. It is best you be off. Likely there'll be more people coming tonight."

He sighed. "Don't worry. I'll help them. Ever since that there messenger of Menno Simons was here, I've never been the same. Seems odd. Had the best crop this year of anybody."

With a light heart, Richard went to the clearing in the Prince-Bishop's woods and settled down to wait for Otto, Trudi, and the others. For a while he curled up and dozed, but awoke at dusk with a strange awareness of someone near him. At first he hoped it was one of the family. He heard heavy breathing, then voices.

"There's no one here," a man said in disgust.

"I saw him come this way, I tell you. This is the Anabaptist secret meeting place I was telling you about. Here he is!"

Before Richard could spring away, a man grabbed him. The bright-colored uniforms and metal helmets of the two men told him they were the Prince-Bishop's soldiers.

"We'll put you in safekeeping and go catch a few more Anabaptists," the first soldier said. "They're streaming out of Munster every day by the dozens."

The two soldiers marched Richard past the friendly farmer's house, past the Church of St. Mauritz, clear back to the encampment by the Mauritz gate. Soldiers in the camp hooted at the little party. "Is that all you got for a night's catch?" one called.

The two soldiers growled a response and led him to a campfire where a woman of the camp stirred a pot of food slung from a tripod.

"Here's a prisoner for you. Keep an eye on him. If he tries to escape, he'll soon find our lances are sharp."

Richard sat near the fire, knees to chin. The food smelled good, but he did not ask for any.

The woman glanced at him and returned to her stirring. "If they're not fighting, they're eating," she grumbled.

"Do you work here?" Richard asked.

The woman snorted. "I certainly do. I'm one of the camp cooks. My husband is one of the Prince-Bishop's men. Mighty small wages he gets for risking his life every day, but at least we eat." She put one hand on her hip. "What were you trying to do?"

"Leave Münster."

"What for? You an Anabaptist trying to escape?" She shoved a bowl of steaming food toward him. "Here, no reason why you should starve. I'll have some, too." She ate with noisy gulps, then yawned. "I'm going to get some sleep. You can stay by the fire, if you want to. But don't try to escape."

Richard sat near the fire and clasped his knees with his hands. Where were Otto and Trudi? Would all the others be caught, too? Were all their plans, all their desires to follow God's Will to come to nothing? He thought of the Anabaptists' secret meetings, where the members spoke in hushed tones of the martyrs who had died for their belief. It had never seemed quite real to him, yet here he was, a prisoner of the Prince-Bishop. True, the Prince-Bishop's soldiers were free-lance, hired to work at soldiering the way other people worked at carpentering, for instance. Perhaps some of them could be bribed.

Richard fingered the coins sewn in his tunic. This money would have to last until he reached

Friesland. But what was he thinking of? He wasn't going anywhere. He was a prisoner. He sighed and drowsed, but woke enough to keep the fire going through the night. In the morning the woman thanked him and let him stir the breakfast porridge.

A soldier came up with a bowl to get his breakfast. "A prisoner, eh? We need a strong boy like you to run errands. How would you like that?"

Alarmed, Richard jumped up. "For the Prince-Bishop? Oh, I couldn't work for him."

"Why not?" The soldier motioned the woman to give Richard some food. "We'll talk this over with the captain over there." He pointed toward a big tent.

"Wait here," he ordered.

Angry voices rose from inside the tent. "Put Mr. Schwartz in chains," a cold voice commanded.

Mr. Schwartz here? Richard sagged with a feeling of hopelessness. Would Mr. Schwartz follow them all until doomsday?

"But why? Why?" Mr. Schwartz pleaded. "I could not help it."

"Take him away. Let the Town Council deal with him."

A soldier flung open the tent flaps. Mr. Schwartz staggered out in the grip of two men. He looked straight at Richard, at first without comprehension, then with a triumphant grin. "There's the boy that did it." Mr. Schwartz wrested himself free and shouted into the tent. "That boy burned the list."

The captain hurried out. "You burned the list yourself."

"But—" Mr. Schwartz floundered and gulped. "But I didn't burn the names. I swear it. The boy did it." Fear and entreaty punctuated Mr. Schwartz' words. "Or maybe it was the other boy."

In spite of himself, Richard felt sorry for Trudi's father. He addressed the captain. "Sir, I—"

The captain silenced him. "Speak when you're spoken to." He waved to the guards.

Mr. Schwartz writhed and pulled, protesting his innocence in a voice that rose in squeaky panic.

The captain grimaced and turned to Richard's guard. "Is this what you call a night's work? One prisoner?"

Richard felt a flutter of delighted hope. Had the others escaped? A sudden elation swept over him. Perhaps some way, with God's help, he could get free and join the family in Friesland. He determined never to give up trying.

The captain motioned Richard inside the tent. "You Anabaptists are strange people. You have a mongrel religion, neither of Rome nor of Martin Luther, just enough truth in it to prove it's from Satan. I understand young people of your age can declare themselves ready for a rebaptism. When were you rebaptized?"

"I haven't been rebaptized," Richard said.

"You haven't? Then what is a good Catholic boy like you doing here?"

A tempting thought occurred to Richard. It would be easy to let the captain think he was a Catholic. In a way, it was true. He had not been rebaptized. Wouldn't it be better to go along with the captain's views? He would be set free,

and he could go on to Friesland. What good could he do as a prisoner? Couldn't God mean for him to accept the mistake of the captain? What better way was there to gain his freedom?

Richard felt hot all over. He wanted to agree with the captain, but then there would be afterward. How could he live with himself? How could he face the new leader, Menno Simons? He would always know what he had done. And then there was Trudi. How could he face her? She who knowingly sacrificed herself to save Richard and his parents? No, it was time that he thought for himself, time that he acted on what he believed.

But you might die—maybe today, the tempter whispered. *How else can you prove your belief in God*, the inner answer came. *The Anabaptists*,

115

*with all their faults, die bravely when called
upon. In one moment you can make up for
months of indecision.*

Richard tried to still the trembling of his
upper lip. "Sir, I am not a Catholic any longer.
I am an Anabaptist, and I plan to be rebaptized
the first chance I get."

12

BELIEVERS IN EXILE

AS soon as he took his stand for God, Richard felt as if a mountain had rolled off his shoulders. He straightened and faced the captain with a light heart.

"But, my boy, don't you realize your words may be your death warrant?"

Richard's newborn confidence did not fail. "Are you going to kill all the Anabaptists?"

The captain stared at Richard. "The Prince-Bishop is not out to kill for killing's sake," he said at last. "He wants law, order, and obedience to the church."

"To the church or to God?" Richard was startled by his own boldness.

The captain sighed. "To God, of course. But I am not going to stay here and argue with a boy all day." He frowned. "Why didn't you let me think you were Catholic? You would be free by now."

"I couldn't. Not now. Besides, it wasn't the truth."

"You knew you might be put to death?"

"Yes."

The captain sighed again. "You Anabaptists have an unshakable courage, I'll surely admit." He drummed his fingers on his sword hilt. "I think I'll send you to the Town Hall. The Town Council can decide what to do with you." He called two guards. "Take him to the Town Hall."

The two guards walked fast. In spite of the sunshine, a chilling wind blew in Richard's face all the way. Near the market place, one of the guards pointed to the high tower of the Church of St. Lamberti. "Look way up there."

Richard looked.

"What do you see?"

"The church tower."

"What else?"

Something in the guard's tone made Richard uneasy. He studied the tower. "I see all the carvings."

"Did you know that six years ago, three of your Anabaptists were put in three cages and strung up there to the tip of the tower and their bones are there yet?"

"No, I didn't know that." An uncontrollable trembling shook Richard. He clenched his teeth. He would not show fear.

"The cages are still there. Look at them," the guard urged.

The command had an irresistible fascination. He found the blackened cages high up on the tower. They seemed like dangling toys.

The guards exchanged small talk until they reached the arcades of the Town Hall. "In you go," one of them told the young prisoner.

A guard on the inside whistled when he saw Richard. "Is this all you can round up today? You should have seen the group that came in yesterday. What's the matter? Are you fattening yourselves on the Prince-Bishop's wages and forgetting your duty?"

One of the guards laughed. "Don't worry. We'll round up enough to keep you busy for a long time to come." He pushed Richard ahead. "The captain says to send him to the Council Room."

"There's a roomful already," the inside guard replied. "However, it's none of my business." He pointed to double doors ahead. "Go over there and rap three times. Someone will take care of you."

The beamed ceilings of the outer room of the Town Hall seemed to close in over Richard. The carved faces on the top of the four stone columns leered at him, yet the golden haze of sunlight from the arched window warmed his whole body. He noticed a stairway at the left and hesitated. Did the council meet upstairs or downstairs?

"Straight ahead, young one," the guard snapped.

At the double doors, Richard knocked three times. He heard a latch click and stepped into a completely dark, boxlike room. What had happened? Was this a cruel joke? Were there dungeons inside the Town Hall? Was he to be imprisoned forever? He blinked at the unaccustomed darkness. Soft daylight glowed from a high, inside window, and Richard saw that he was between two sets of double doors. What was he supposed to do? He fumbled ahead and felt a slanted iron knocker in the middle of the door just ahead; he pushed it. Someone on the other side opened the door.

He stood at one side of a big, oblong room surrounded on three sides by wooden benches, each one backed by a carved panel of wood. Straight ahead, soft daylight poured through the leaded windows. A movement behind him made him turn. A group of people stood waiting. It took but a moment for Richard to recognize Father, Mother, Uncle Sigmund, Aunt Frieda, Otto, and Trudi. He gasped and looked again. All were there, smiling encouragement. Two guards stood with pikes pointing ceilingward.

A rustle in the outer hall stiffened Richard.

The councilmen filed in and took their places in the wooden seats. Here and there a councilman adjusted purple or green cushions behind his back. The presiding officer took his place behind a long desk with five carved panels. When the men sat down, the presiding officer opened the meeting.

"Who has anything against these folks?"

There was another rustle at the door. Mr. Schwartz swept in with head high. "I have."

"What is your claim?"

"These people have been rabid Anabaptists for years." Mr. Schwartz' wave included the whole group. "There are two brothers, as you can see, and their two sons. I myself helped stone the one brother out of Munster months ago, yet you see him here. The other became affiliated with the Anabaptists and was excommunicated."

Mr. Schwartz warmed up to his own talking. "Not only that, but this man's son destroyed a list of names that would have been of great value to the council—names of Anabaptists still infecting Münster." Mr. Schwartz paraded in front of the councilmen, swinging his arms and gesturing. "The worst thing of all—they burned down the house of the Prince-Bishop."

Mr. Schwartz' boldness infuriated Richard. A hot denial burned on his lips, but he held himself in check. Trudi, however, burst past the guards.

"Father, you lie."

A murmur ran around the seated councilmen. The presiding officer rapped for silence. "Who is this girl?"

Mr. Schwartz, with a stricken look, let his hands drop to his sides. "My daughter."

"Why is she with these people?"

Mr. Schwartz started to explain.

"She will speak for herself. Let us understand why these Anabaptists act as they do."

Trudi stood tense and straight. "I am following God's will."

"But to do so, you must be a good Catholic. Do you not see the error of your ways?"

"God's Will is not an error."

In spite of the presiding officer's probing questions, Trudi stood firm.

Mr. Schwartz broke in. "The city must rid itself of these heretics or we will be endangered as we were six years ago."

The presiding officer glared at him. "Does this include your own daughter?"

"Yes, of course. She must be punished, too. No—no. What am I saying?" Mr. Schwartz reeled and put a hand to his head. "Perhaps they could be banished."

The presiding officer raised his hand. "It will be the judgment of the council, not of a layman, to determine what punishment shall be meted out." He turned to the councilmen. "Does anyone have a word to say in defense of these people?"

A burgher spoke up. "I have had many fine carved pieces of furniture from these men. Both are good craftsmen."

122   Another leaned forward and glared at the first speaker. Richard could see that the carving behind his chair showed the figure of Christ carrying an orb. "Wolves ought to be killed," he said. "The Anabaptists are wolves."

"The Anabaptists praise God when they are mistreated," a third man mused. "They joyfully die for their religion. There must be something wrong with such people. They say such good and pious things of God that they must be bad."

The presiding officer held up his hand for attention. "Did these people have any banned books on them?"

"No, Your Honor."

"What do they have to say for themselves? Let me hear their defense."

Uncle Sigmund stepped forward. "Christ said to let the wheat grow with the tares until the time of harvest, lest while ye gather up the tares ye root up also the wheat with them. We cannot ignore the Word of God. We serve Him, live for Him, and if need be, we will die for Him who died for us."

"Do the rest of you agree to this?" the presiding officer asked.

Richard felt a strength he never thought was possible. His "Yes," was as loud and firm as the others.

"The council decrees banishment from Münster for the Janssen family forever. No member may return here again. They may never come through the gates either to trade, to buy, to sell, or to work. They may never break bread in anyone's house or sleep therein." The presiding officer intoned the sentence, pronouncing each word with care. "As for Hugo Schwartz, let him continue to live in the parish of St. Mauritz, but let him offer confession each Friday at the Church of St. Lamberti for the rest of his natural life, lest his zeal lead him to take the law into his own hands."

Hugo Schwartz bowed his head, and with a last long look at Trudi, he left the council room.

In a few moments several guards rounded up the family and escorted them to the Mauritz gate. In silence the guards at the gate allowed them to pass through. The gates of the city clanged shut behind them. The Janssen family had been banished from Münster forever.

Richard, Otto, and Trudi trudged side by side. When they passed the old familiar places, the Church of St. Mauritz, the farmhouses of former friends and neighbors, and above all, the distant woods which sheltered the secret church, a secret no longer now that it was in the Prince-Bishop's hands, Richard felt as if his heart would burst with sadness, and yet a newborn joy quickened within him. A new life lay ahead.

Trudi looked back. "Oh, how I wish Father could see the light," she sighed. She never looked back again.

The long days of walking brought their own peace. Trudi kept pointing out misty blues and greens of far-off hills, the deep dip of a river, clusters of houses at the top of a rise, or an entire town on a hillside. The beauty of nature seemed to lay a soothing hand on everyone.

Every night there was the adventure of finding a place to sleep and eat. Many times a kind farmer let them sleep on hay with the cattle. People shared food, and often had to be almost forced to accept money.

Weeks later in the flat countryside of Friesland, with its many canals, the Janssen party settled in the little town where Menno Simons lived. Father and Uncle Sigmund soon found themselves in demand as carpenters. At first

124

Father and Uncle Sigmund cautioned the family not to mention Menno Simons' name, but as soon as everyone learned the new language, Father decided to make inquiries.

Richard went with him on the first attempt. Near a canal Father stopped a passerby.

"Where can we find Menno Simons?"

"Menno Simons?" The man gave a queer little jump and looked over his shoulder. "I couldn't say, I'm sure."

"But surely, you must have heard of him. Word has spread of his fame throughout the northern countries."

"No, no, I beg of you, do not mention that name. You cannot tell what will happen now. We are all watched."

Father called out in a cautious voice to another passerby, "Peace be with thee."

The man turned, raising his hand slowly as if to ward off blows. He studied Father and Richard. "Who are you?" he said at last.

"We are newcomers here."

"From whence?"

"From Münster."

"Why do you come here?"

"We seek a man who will help us."

"What is his name?"

"Menno Simons."

The man jerked back and swallowed hard. "Do you not know that the name Menno Simons is forbidden here?"

"Is there persecution?"

"Aye. Don't you know the law?"

"No."

The man sighed. "The governor of Friesland

decreed last year on December 7, 1542, that anyone who gave food or lodging to Menno Simons is liable to heresy. My advice is for you to go elsewhere."

"No, we shall not go on until we have found him," Father said.

The man brooded. "These days there are spies everywhere."

"I understand," Father said. "We will trouble you no further. Peace be with you."

"Wait." The man brooded for a moment. "You have given the greeting of the Brethren. I will take you to Menno Simons."

He took them to a little house near a canal. Menno Simons was writing messages to be printed for his followers.

"Here are some seekers of light from Münster."

A cloud passed over the serene face of Menno Simons. "I have worried about those in Münster, although I have never been in Münster in all my life."

Richard gazed into the quiet, serene face of the man they had walked so far to meet and knew that all would be well.

Once again the secret meetings began.

Menno Simons reminded his followers often, "Soon shall come the day of our refreshing and all the tears shall be wiped from our eyes. Praise God and lift up your heads, ye who suffer for Jesus' sake."

He did not like to hear the word *Anabaptists*. At one meeting he chided his followers. "We must rid ourselves of this name of Anabaptists. It is a hateful title, one we never chose. Hereafter we call ourselves "the Brethren."

After the meeting Richard whispered to Trudi. "Let's ask to be baptized."

That night he, Otto, and Trudi stood with the Brethren by the side of a canal and waited for the baptism.

"Baptism does not confer grace," Menno Simons explained. "It is a divine ordinance which marks the spiritual rebirth of a Christian."

He baptized Trudi first, Otto next, and then Richard. At that moment, Richard felt as if light poured inside his head. "It isn't the water that matters," he told himself. "It's what the water stands for."

Then he understood the secret church of the Brethren, a church, first of all, in his own heart, and in the hearts of each of the others. It was the true church. Exhilarated, filled with new strength and hope, he looked at Trudi and Otto. From the quiet joy on their faces, Richard knew they had made the same discovery as he.

The Author

Louise A. Vernon was born in Coquille, Oregon. As children, her grandparents crossed the Great Plains in covered wagons. After graduating from Willamette University, she studied music and creative writing, which she taught in the San Jose public schools.

In her series of religious-heritage juveniles, Vernon recreates for children events and figures from church history in Reformation times. She has traveled in England and Germany, researching firsthand the settings for her fictionalized real-life stories. In each book she places a child on the scene with the historical character and involves the child in an exciting plot. The National Association of Christian Schools honored *Ink on His Fingers* as one of the two best children's books with a Christian message released in 1972.